Community of Women

LAWRENCE BLOCK
writing as Sheldon Lord

COMMUNITY OF WOMEN

LAWRENCE BLOCK writing as SHELDON LORD

Copyright © 1961 Lawrence Block

All Rights Reserved.

Cover and Interior Design by QA Productions

A LAWRENCE BLOCK PRODUCTION

CLASSIC EROTICA

---

21 Gay Street
Candy
Gigolo Johnny Wells
April North
Carla
A Strange Kind of Love
Campus Tramp
Community of Women
Born to be Bad
College for Sinners
Of Shame and Joy
A Woman Must Love
The Adulterers
The Twisted Ones
High School Sex Club
I Sell Love
69 Barrow Street
Four Lives at the Crossroads
Circle of Sinners
A Girl Called Honey
Sin Hellcat
So Willing

CLASSIC EROTICA #8

COMMUNITY OF WOMEN

Lawrence Block

CHAPTER 1

The alarm clock rang at precisely fourteen minutes to seven. It was an electric clock that had been painfully acquired at the cost of several months' worth of trading stamps accumulated from a gas station, a supermarket and a dry-cleaner. Since Howard Haskell invariably forgot to wind alarm clocks, this electric clock was a blessing of sorts. Power failures, not uncommon in Cheshire Point, tended to negate its value, having once conspired to deliver Howard at the offices of MacNaughton and Byrnes at 12:15 in the afternoon. But this morning there was no power failure. The alarm clock once again proved a blessing, exploding into noise at, as has been noted, precisely fourteen minutes before seven o'clock.

Nan Haskell didn't think of it as a blessing. Before her eyes were entirely open her hand reached out from beneath the covers, her forefinger unerringly headed for the button which would turn off the clock. Then, the ringing stilled, she permitted herself the luxury of one yawn. Her whole body stretched beneath the covers like a giant cat uncoiling at a fireside. It was a pleasure to stretch, she thought. A pleasure to come awake slowly, gingerly, entering the land of wakefulness like a reluctant swimmer stepping into cold water.

A pleasure she couldn't afford. Grimly she swung her legs

over the edge of the bed, stood up, blinked her blue eyes groggily. Howard was still asleep, or pretending to be; she reached over and shook his shoulder, squeezing him with the natural intimacy of wife for husband. She did not say a word. Long experience had taught her that anyone who said a word to Howard Haskell before he had his morning coffee was asking for trouble. He opened his eyes, got out of bed, and Nan headed for the bathroom.

She had no time for a shower. That would come later, when Howard was off to the advertising agency and the kids were on their way to school. Until then she could not waste a moment. She washed her face with cold water, flapped a toothbrush over her teeth. She went back to the bedroom, wrapped a housecoat around her, and headed downstairs to make breakfast.

Even at that ungodly hour of the morning, with the shapeless housecoat around her, with her hair uncombed and her head still foggy from the last martini of the night before, Nan Haskell was a striking woman. She was tall and full-bodied, with long corn-yellow hair and a Hollywood figure. Firm full breasts pushed out the front of the housecoat. The belt, which she had tied carelessly, was snug around a narrow waist. Her hips were also full and sensual, and as she shuffled around the kitchen in house-slippers they still swayed in a distinctly physical manner.

The morning went as weekday mornings always went. Howard entered the breakfast nook at the precise moment that the orange juice and eggs and toast and coffee hit the table. His hair was cropped in a crew-cut, his narrow tie neatly knotted, his skin glowing with the deceptive vitality induced under a sunlamp. He sat down, ate wordlessly, drank his coffee, set fire to the tip of the day's first Pall Mall, and then, finally, smiled and returned to the land of the living.

"Good coffee," he said.

For four years now, these had been the first words Nan Haskell heard five mornings out of every seven. She replied by asking him if the eggs were all right. She always asked Howard if the eggs were all right. They always were.

"Better get going," he said. "Want to run me down to the station?"

"Glad to. Everything set?"

"Everything. The Old Man wants the Dunridge presentation today. I've got a portfolio ready that ought to set the old bastard on his ear."

Nan had no idea what the Dunridge presentation was. Howard had never told her. She said that was fine, and he picked up his slim attaché case, and she wrapped the housecoat a little tighter around herself, and they went to the car.

There were two cars. The one they took to the Cheshire Point station of the New York, New Haven and Hartford Rail Road was the station wagon. It was a Chevy, five years old, roomy, economical, and paid for. The other car, which remained in the attached garage of their split-level colonial home, was a Cadillac sedan. It was new, shiny, expensive to operate, too long for the garage, and not paid for. Howard had once calculated that the Caddy would be fully paid for at about the time that Skip, their six-year-old, was ready to enter Junior High. They tried not to think about that little fact too often.

Nan dropped her husband at the station, watched him walk up onto the platform with a cigarette in his hand, waiting for the 8:03 to wend its wayward way into the station. She glanced around, watching other wives kiss other husbands goodbye for the day, all of them synchronizing their little lives to fit the schedules of the New York, New Haven and Hartford Rail Road. There was something about the whole thing, something that had made Nan wince uncomfortably from time to time. All the wives in housecoats, all the husbands in flannel suits, all the copies of the *Times* or the *Trib* in the hands of all the men, all the dangling attaché cases—

She didn't have time to think about it. She put the car in gear and headed back to the split-level colonial, a rather strange architectural concept which was in great demand in that particular area of northern Westchester County. She parked in the driveway, entered the house, woke the kids and started cooking the second breakfast of the day.

Danny, who was eight, tried to argue that he had enough of a cold to keep him out of school.

"You're going to school," she told him.

"Aw, Mom—"

"Your father pays twenty-five dollars a month in school tax," she told him. "We go to meeting of the PTA on the average of three times a month. You are going to school, Danny Boy."

"Aw, Mom—"

She drove them both to school in the station wagon. At precisely fourteen minutes before nine, exactly two hours after the dreadful ringing of the dreadful alarm clock, she kissed both boys goodbye and watched them creeping like snails unwillingly to school. Other mothers were doing the same with other children, and Nan looked at them and thought of the similarity between this little scene and the scene at the railway station. It was funny, but it was too early in the morning to laugh. Besides, she had thought similar thoughts often enough in the past.

The station wagon made the return trip to the split-level colonial and placed the car, this time, alongside the Cadillac in the garage. She went into the house, ate breakfast herself, finally, and went upstairs to stand under the shower. The pelting spray of hot water on her bare flesh made her fully awake for the first time. She had never been able to come alive without a shower in the morning. It was a habit begun long before marriage, before her job as an editorial assistant at Greybarr Publications, before her four years at Clifton College. A shower, something to wash off a night of sleep and a day before—

She rubbed herself briskly with a nubby pink towel, rubbed herself until her skin tingled and her nerve ends vibrated with life. She dressed, putting on a plaid skirt and a simple white blouse.

After the beds were made, she wandered downstairs and poured out a fresh cup of coffee. She took it to the living room and sat down in a Danish modern chair, sleek and simple and incredibly uncomfortable. She rested the cup of coffee in its saucer on the freeform cherrywood coffee table and lighted a cigarette.

She thought of other wives in Cheshire Point. She thought of all the husbands on the 8:03 to Grand Central, and of all the children now at their desks in various levels of the Cheshire Point public education system. And all the wives, alone.

A whole little community of women, she thought. All our brats are in school and all our husbands are in the city. And we sit home alone all day until the kids and husbands drift home. What in the name of God Almighty do we do with ourselves?

She finished the cigarette and the coffee. She, of course, had things to do—a house to clean, shopping to shop for, people to call and odds and ends to take care of. Never a dull moment in Cheshire Point. Wait a minute, she thought. Correct that. Plenty of dull moments, but never an occupied one. Loads of monotony, oodles of banality, an impressive quantity of boredom.

And here we are, Nan thought. Thirty-two years old, pretty, married, two kids, and an expensive and ugly heavily-mortgaged house on a full-acre plot in lovely Cheshire Point. And a day full of monotony with the boys in school and Howard on Madison Avenue.

Was this what she had wanted? Was this the dream stuff in Clifton College, where she had majored in English and covered reams of unlined yellow paper with sophomoric poetry? Was this the dream at Greybarr, where she waded through the slush pile, pinning Thanks But No Thanks notes on manuscripts from frustrated Iowa housewives? Was this the be-all and end-all, the obvious role for an intelligent woman in the twentieth century?

Cheshire Point. Close enough to New York so the men could get to work, far enough away so the air was clean and the grounds were spacious and the schools were good. Country advantages and city convenience—that was the sales pitch, and it was true enough, fundamentally.

She ground out a cigarette, stood up, stretched. There was nothing wrong with Cheshire Point, she told herself. It was better than a Manhattan apartment, better than a sandbox house in Queens, better than the real country. It was the best they could possibly afford, and she was perfectly satisfied with it.

Wasn't she?

She thought again of all the other women in all the other houses in Cheshire Point. Women alone, she thought romantically. Women alone, with the menfolk away. Might make a thoughtful article for a woman's mag, maybe the one with the togetherness pitch. Or, with a little sex tossed in, a hot item for the exposé type books. *Sin In The Suburbs*. Or *Excitement In The Exurbs*. Or—

Things to do, shopping and cleaning and straightening up. Was the evening free? No, she thought sadly, it wasn't. The Carrs, Ted and Elly, were due to arrive for an evening of family bridge. Not that she didn't like the Carrs, but it would be heaven to spend an evening alone with Howie for a change instead of sharing his company with the rest of the world.

At eleven-thirty, after a trip to the Grand Union and after a load of wash had gone first into washing machine and then into dryer, she thought again about Sin In The Suburbs and Excitement In The Exurbs. No, she thought; no article there. What kind of sin could happen in Cheshire Point?

Hardly a nest of sinful folk. Take Elly Carr, for example. Now who in the name of God Almighty could imagine Elly, for example, cheating on her husband?

CHAPTER 2

It was twelve-thirty in the afternoon, and Elly Carr was about to cheat on her husband.

She had done this before. She was a very attractive woman, two years younger than Nan Haskell and several inches shorter. Her hair was black, and she wore it in an Italian-style haircut which made her look perhaps three years younger than she was. Her build was boyish, while distinctly feminine; men who lusted for Audrey Hepburn were frequently entranced by Elly Carr. Her breasts were small but firm and well-shaped, her waist very slender, her hips barely evident.

She had one child, a dark-haired pug-nosed girl named Pamela. Pam was at school now, not due to return until three-thirty. She had a husband named Ted, a sandy-haired public relations executive. Ted was in an air-conditioned office on Forty-eighth Street off Madison, not due to return until six-fifteen. She had, then, a minimum of three hours to cheat on her husband.

It rarely took that long.

Her partner now was a man named Rudy Gerber. He was the deliveryman for the dry cleaner, a husky fellow about twenty-five years old with an athletic build and a handsome if ruggedly stupid face. He had made love to her a week before. Now he was about to make love to her again.

Elly didn't love Rudy Gerber. She didn't even especially *like* Rudy Gerber, as far as that went. But that had nothing to do with it. Rudy Gerber was quite excellent in bed, and Elly was randy as a brood mare in the springtime, and the bed was ready, and what the hell. God was in his heaven, all was about as right with the world as it ever was, and she was going to get loved.

So what the hell.

"I been looking forward to this," Rudy Gerber said. "Last week—I mean, something like this don't happen all the time. A broad like you—"

He let the sentence trail off. It was a habit of his, as though his mind couldn't hold too much and it was enough of an effort to begin a sentence, much less complete it. She wished he would talk less. He talked so stupidly that the words only tended to spoil things.

But she said: "You must meet lots of lonely women."

"Well," he said. He scratched his head and leered, trying to look like a man of the world and not quite succeeding.

"This way, Rudy."

She led him up a long flight of stairs. The house, unlike the Haskell home, was an older structure, one of the original homes in the town of Cheshire Point. It was an authentic center hall colonial, complete with hand-hewn exposed beams and loads of rustic charm. That had been the salesman's strongest selling point, and Ted had gone for it hook, line and thirty-year mortgage. He liked to fancy himself a Colonial type, or Edwardian at the very least. A colonial house fit into his sublime image of himself, along with the tweed jackets and the pipe and the foreign car.

They went into the bedroom. Rudy Gerber grinned. "Some broad you are," he said. "Some hell of a broad."

"You Tarzan," she said.

He stared at her.

"You Tarzan," she repeated. "Me Jane. That bed. Let's get with it, sweetheart."

They got with it. He reached for her, lunging a little like Tarzan and a little like an anthropoid ape, and she let his big ape-arms close around her slender body and draw her close. She smelled the strong man-smell of him, the fresh sweat and the dirty clothes that could have used his employer's attention. And that did it. The sarcasm and the cynicism left her. She was a woman in heat now, a woman who needed a man.

She reached upward, throwing her arms around his neck and hugging him. Her mouth ground against his mouth and her tongue snaked into his mouth. She felt the immediate urgency of his response, felt him quicken with desire and go rigid with need for her, and her body grew warmer with knowledge of her sure appeal.

They were on the bed then, suddenly, and his hand was on her breast. She felt his fingers fondling her, felt dizzying sensations racing through her system. She was a woman now, a woman, a woman with a man. Everything else disappeared.

He took off her blouse. His hands found her breasts again, played with them. She shivered with tremendous delight, the excitement moving within her body like a living entity. His hands went around her, impatient now, struggling with the bra. He broke the clasp and wrenched the bra off, exposing her breasts.

Their love play was deliberate and intense. He handled and

kissed her breasts and she began to pant volcanically, Vesuvius in the throes of an eruption. Her eyes were closed and her hips were already churning in the mystic motions of love. She was on fire.

He stroked her and kissed her. She lay with her eyes closed, imagining not Rudy Gerber but a phantom lover, a man on a sleek black stallion, a man dressed in black with eyes like pools of black fire. A man who would whisper poetry to her, a man who would kiss her when she was good and whip her when she was bad. A man who would always be master and for whom she would be forever a willing slave.

A phantom lover.

She was on the bed, squirming. She was on the bed, wearing black toreador pants that were tight on her slim hips, and Rudy was taking them off. He had trouble with the zipper, mastered it, and then had trouble with the pants themselves. Finally they were off, and then the wispy panties were also off, and he was catching his breath at the sight of her milk-white naked body. His large hands raced over her bare flesh, setting her tingling, making her skin burn with liquid heat.

He threw himself down on her, kissed her. His tongue was the aggressor now, stabbing joltingly into her mouth. He squeezed a breast in one hand and a thigh in the other and her brain burned with feverish heat.

Phantom lover.

He let go of her to fumble with his own clothing. His big hands tore his tee-shirt over his head, unbelted his dungarees, pulled them down. He was heavy, with a beer-belly developing, with flab on his upper arms. But she did not notice all those things because her eyes were closed. She was not seeing Rudy Gerber now. She was seeing the phantom lover. He had dismounted from his black stallion. He was coming toward her—

Rudy took her. He took her as a stallion takes a randy brood mare in the springtime, fell upon her and possessed her, using her body with an almost vicious passion.

And now, in her mind, she was with that phantom lover. Rudy's panting was the music of the hills and the groans of the bedsprings were wind in tall grasses. She was with her phantom lover, riding close behind him on the black stallion, riding far from the rest of the world.

Faster.

Faster—

Rudy, panting like a truck horse. The odor of sweat, the odor of lust being consummated, the odor of sex in a Cheshire Point master bedroom. The odor of noonday lust.

Faster . . ..

And then the culmination. The orgasm, the peak of pleasure, with a thunderous crash that jolted her and left her limp. The End, Finis, #, —30—, *that's all, folks.*

He got up slowly, his eyes hollow, his breathing coming in gasps. He got up and looked at her, and she opened her eyes to see the vulgar animal stare focusing on her bare body. Instinctively she drew a sheet over herself, up to her neck, as if to prevent him from looking at what he had so recently possessed.

"Go," she said. Just that.

"Next week?"

She looked at him, looked away. "Just go," she said.

She stayed in bed until she heard the door close downstairs. She stayed in bed until she heard the panel truck pull away from the curb, carrying within it a load of clothing to be dry-cleaned and a man who had just made love to her. Then she hurried from the bed to the shower, washing the memory of Rudy Gerber from her skin. She spent twenty minutes under the shower. When she stepped from the tub she felt almost clean again.

She changed the bed linen.

By one-thirty she was in the kitchen, drinking coffee and smoking a filter-tipped cigarette. She had done it again, had had another meaningless affair with another meaningless man. She had sinned; she should wear a red A upon her left breast so all the world would know her as the adulteress she was.

Suddenly she laughed. A scarlet letter—maybe that would fit Ted's magnificent image! After all, they weren't that far from New England. And that was Nathaniel Hawthorne country. Why, she could be sort of a latter-day Hester Prynne, a twentieth-century adulteress who went for every male within laying distance.

Why?

Dammit, why?

It had always been this way. Elly Carr was a New York girl, in contrast to the typical exurban wife who began life as a Midwestern product, went from college to Manhattan, and wound up in a house in Westchester or Rockland or Fairfield or Bucks. Elly had been born on West 73rd Street near Broadway, had gone to New York schools and Hunter College. She had lost her virginity in her sophomore year at Evander Childs High to a now-forgotten member of the football team, had sacrificed that tiny membrane on her living room couch while her parents lay sleeping in the bedroom.

And she had been an easy make ever since. All you had to do

was be husky and masculine and stupid and willing and good ol' Elly Barshter would be flat on her back with her knees in the air. The football team had enjoyed her, and the swimming squad had enjoyed her, and the track team, and the baseball team—

College had not changed her, but it had edged her with subtlety. In high school, everybody knew she was an easy make. In college, the only ones who knew this were the ones who had been to bed with her. After college, when she was pounding the typewriter at Berman and Bates, she never slept with any of the men who worked in the office. She laughed with them, and she joked with them, and she went to shows and concerts with them. But she slept with raw-boned dockworkers that she picked up in sleazy bars.

She hadn't slept with Ted, not until he married her and whisked her away to New Hampshire on a honeymoon. Then she came into his arms, as virginal as possible, and if he knew there had been men before him he never told her. And she was going to be true to him—she swore to it herself a thousand times, told herself again and again that he was the only man for her, that she had helled around enough and that it was now time to settle down and be a good wife to a good husband.

It wasn't that hard in New York. They had an apartment on a quiet street in one of the better sections of Greenwich Village, and she kept her job at Berman and Bates, and things were fine. She was with Ted every minute possible, and he was an ardent lover and she needed him desperately. There were no other men then. There was no time for other men, and no need for other men, and she was true to Ted.

Then all at once she was pregnant. The pregnancy was

accidental, but this fact made her no less pregnant. And New York was no place to raise kids, and Ted was making good money, and his dream included an old house in the wilds of Westchester, and after a long search they found the right place with the right sort of grounds and the right layout.

And they moved to Cheshire Point.

She had the baby. Pam took a great deal of time at first, and again she was true to Ted, faithful to Ted, a good wife. Because there was no time for infidelity. She dreamed the same dreams of a phantom lover but nothing came of them.

Time changed that. Time sent Pam to school. Time gave her hours by herself, hours alone in the house, with deliverymen calling and salesmen calling and finally, finally—

It happened. And once it happened—with a nameless faceless man she had long since forgotten—it was easy enough for the pattern to repeat itself, to establish itself, to become part of her life. She was once again the easy lay, the easy make, the gal who dreamed of a phantom lover on a black stallion and gave herself to every brawny clod who knocked on the door.

Ted did not know. No one knew, no one but the countless men who had made a Hester Prynne of her. And Ted would not know, not if she could possibly avoid it. Because she loved Ted.

Yet she went on cheating on him.

She left the kitchen, walked through the house. She looked at the living room fireplace, looked at the exposed hand-hewn beams.

Why?

Dammit, why?

CHAPTER 3

Late afternoon in Cheshire Point. A hot day, with the sun high in the sky to the west and only a few stray cirrus clouds breaking the expanse of blue. Nan Haskell had finished what housework had to be done. There was a roast in the oven; the rest of the meal could wait. Skip and Danny had both gravitated to other backyards to play with other children. Nan sat at her desk, going over some of the household bookkeeping which had become her responsibility since they had moved to Cheshire Point. That had been Howard's job in Manhattan, but with him spending eight hours a day on the job and three hours more commuting, it had gravitated to her shoulders.

Late afternoon in Cheshire Point. Somewhere someone was burning leaves and the rich smoke hung in the fresh country air. Elly Carr stretched out on a chaise on the lawn in back of her home and smelled the smoke. Pam was upstairs, playing with her dolls or something of the sort. Elly had picked her up after school, but somehow she couldn't manage to spend any time with her daughter on those days when she had had a lover. Shower or not, she still felt fundamentally unclean. Pam, with her glossy dark hair and her pug nose, was the perfect symbol of innocence. Elly felt almost as though her own presence would contaminate the girl. It was on days like this one that she most wanted to be with

Pamela, and it was paradoxically on these days that she had to remain most within herself. She stretched out on the chaise and thought about bridge with the Haskells, which she dreaded tonight, and dinner, which she did not want to prepare. Well, she could always chuck a few TV dinners in the oven—

Late afternoon in Cheshire Point. A breeze was blowing up from the southeast, coming up off Long Island and the Atlantic. Trees swayed in the breeze, and loose autumn leaves were wafted by it. Roz Barclay sat in her garden in a wicker chair and thought about money.

Money.

In every exurb there are three classes of persons. First there are the natives, those souls whose families lived in the town from the beginning, and who now make their livelihood from the recent immigrants. These persons, like Rudy Gerber, for example, run the stores that the immigrants patronize and perform various services for the new arrivals. They tend to consider New Yorkers a breed apart, even though those New Yorkers may have resided in the exurb for ten or fifteen years.

Then there are the commuters, families like the Haskells and the Carrs. For the most part, they earn their livings in that complex of advertising and publishing and public relations and television which falls under the general heading of communications. They belong to the exurb and to New York, living in one place and working in the other.

And, finally, there are the geniuses.

Linc Barclay was a genius. A genius, in exurban terminology, is a New Yorker living in the exurb who does not have to commute. A genius may be a commercial artist or a composer or a dramatist. He may, like Lincoln Barclay, be a writer. He lives in Cheshire Point, works at home, and goes to New York at odd intervals because New York is, ultimately, the source of his income, the market for his wares. Shows are produced there, books and magazines are published there—so he lives close to the city, but does not commute. He is thus a breed apart from the nine-to-five crowd.

Lincoln Barclay was a commercial writer. He sold stories to slick magazines, for which he was paid anywhere from one to three thousand dollars, and he wrote novels for a variety of paperback publishers, for which he was paid in the neighborhood of twenty-five hundred dollars plus royalties.

And his wife, a pretty girl with dark brown hair and a willowy figure, sat in a wicker chair and thought about money.

Roz drew on her cigarette. Genius or not, Linc was in New York today. He'd gone into town to see his agent in a desperate attempt to cadge still another advance against future sales. There had already been a great number of advances against future sales. And, because it had been a matter of months since there had been anything of note accomplished on the IBM electric typewriter in the clapboard guest house Linc used for a study, those nebulous future sales seemed very nebulous, and very much in the future.

Linc was in a slump. It was a bad slump, the worst so far in a life composed of hot periods and slumps alternating precariously. The typewriter was silent, Linc was moody, and the cycle was vicious. He had been halfway through a paperback novel when the slump hit and the contract had called for delivery of the book weeks ago. The publisher was impatient, the agent was impatient, and now, with income at a standstill and bills piling up, the creditors were becoming impatient.

Roz sighed. She yawned unhappily, her large breasts drawn into sharp relief against her red jersey shirt. She took a deep breath and let it out slowly. It was hell being a writer, she thought. It was even hell being married to a writer. Oh, it was fine when the good times came—she thought of that time when Warner Brothers bought *Naked By Moonlight* out of the blue and dropped thirty-five thousand dollars into Linc's lap. And then the trip to Europe, and the new car, and—

Those were the good times. And not having to commute, not playing a role in the Ulcer Gulch rat-race, that was good. Being your own boss, working your own hours, planning your own life—those were good things. But the ad men and the PR boys didn't have to worry about slumps. They could get laid off, they could get dumped with little ceremony, and their jobs were by no means secure. But they never had the awful feeling of a writer in a slump, the feeling of a man trying to draw water from a dry well. The horrible feeling when there were no words to type on sheets of paper, no words at all.

They could go dry, or stale, and the money still came in every week. They knew just how much was coming in, could budget expenses and plan ahead and know where the money was coming from. They might overspend themselves, but at least they had the chance to plan.

Not so with Linc. Not so, because he never knew what month would be a good month financially and what month would be a catastrophe. Even without a slump, they could find themselves in a cash bind, with a host of sales in the Soon-To-Be-Paid file and no dough in the checking account. And when a long slump hit—

There were no children. That kept a certain ceiling on expenditures. But there were the mortgage payments on the house, the monthly payments on the car, the insurance payments, the gas bill, the electric bill, the taxes, the phone bill, a whole bevy of fixed costs before they even got around to putting food on the table. And you couldn't cut your personal expenses too far. You had to keep up a front for the neighbors, had to make a certain pretense of economic security. You had to entertain now and then, had to find money somewhere to buy expensive liquor for other people to drink. Whether you could afford it or not.

No money coming in, and money always going out. Linc was advanced to the hilt. He owed his agent three thousand dollars, and was now doing his damnedest to wangle another thousand. That meant four thousand dollars' worth of work before he would see more money. Two books, say.

And the slump was still going strong.

She ground out her cigarette in the grass, sucking in a mouthful of air and struggling to keep the tears back. God, how she loved Linc! She never regretted marrying him, not even in the bad times, *especially* not in the bad times. These were the times when he needed her, when she had to reassure him that the slump would end, that every cloud had that silly silver lining, that he would write his way out of debt and out of whatever weird and unknowable personal hell was causing the slump in the first place. He needed her, needed the love and consolation she could give him.

And she needed him.

Emotionally, because helping her man and sticking by her man were things which made Roz aware of her own essential femininity. And physically as well, because she was a passionate woman, a woman who surrendered her whole being to the sexual embrace of the man she loved. She had been a virgin until Linc made a woman of her in a sagging bed at a rundown motel across the Putnam County line, and since that night no other man had ever held her in his arms. She needed Linc, needed him most of all during the bad times when the slump was at its worst and the typewriter was silent and the bank balance dwindled away.

Which was markedly unfortunate.

Because when Lincoln Barclay had a slump, he had a slump. And such a slump was more than a professional matter. It was a sexual matter as well. Something other than his production of prose drooped.

A woman less fundamentally monogamous might have taken a lover. A woman less sensual might have suffered in silence. Roz Barclay found another outlet, a reversion to the habits of adolescence, a temporary measure that relieved the need for sex better than nothing at all.

And now was time for it. Now, with Linc in New York for the next hour or two, with the house to herself, with no pressing obligation but the relief of her own sexual needs.

She got up from the wicker chair and walked slowly toward the back door of the house. She was trembling, less in delighted anticipation than from the anxieties that always were the muted accompaniment of self-satisfaction. Guilt was an inevitable by-product. She knew, intellectually if not emotionally, that there was no reason to feel guilty, that what she was about to do was neither immoral nor harmful, that it was neither an act of infidelity nor a pernicious habit. Yet the guilt remained; society had its own ideas, and her heart accepted what her mind could manage to reject.

She went to the bathroom on the second floor. This, too, was habit, an obvious carry-over from teenage years when the bathroom had been the place for every secret vice from cigarette smoking to what she was going to do now. The bedroom might have been more comfortable, but the bathroom was the inevitable place, seated upon the toilet with the door securely locked.

She sat down, closed the door, turned the lock. She shut her eyes, and in the ensuing darkness her own hands roamed her body. Her own guilty hands stroked her full breasts, reached beneath the bra to cup firm flesh and fondle the nipples that were already stiffening with lust. She unhooked the bra, releasing her breasts, and she prodded their softness while her brain began to whirl with the fantasies of sex, with memories of nights in Linc's arms, with sexual dreams and sexual themes.

No!

She couldn't. It was wrong, it was impossible and she couldn't. No!

Slowly, dizzily, she rearranged her clothing and got to her feet. Her fingers found the lock, turned it. She left the bathroom and went downstairs once again.

The frustration was alive now. It was a living breathing pulsating force within her and she fought it with every bit of strength in her body. She breathed in gasps, struggling to pull herself together. Other women would find a way out. Other women would play around. But she had to be true, true to Linc and true to herself.

Even if it killed her. Even if it had her climbing the damned walls, for God's sake—

It was late afternoon in Cheshire Point.

CHAPTER 4

It was night in Cheshire Point.

It was a relatively dark night, as a matter of complete fact. The moon was a thin crescent hardly there at all. A cloud cover had blown in from the east and the stars were few and far between. This, however, is relatively immaterial. The Carrs and the Haskells, busy playing bridge at the Haskell colonial-split, were in the basement recreation room, seated around a card table. It hardly mattered whether the moon was full or not, whether the sky was bright or dark.

What mattered, Nan Haskell thought, was that Ted Carr was making passes at her.

To give Ted full credit, they were remarkably subtle passes. When you are sitting at a bridge table with your own wife, and with another man and his wife, you have to go some in order to make passes at the other man's wife without anyone else realizing the fact. But Nan knew damned well that Ted Carr was a past master at the art of the subtle forward pass. It was, she thought, one hell of a shame that a decent, straight-and-narrow girl like Elly should be married to a philanderer like Ted Carr.

While Elly sat quietly in the background, very neat and very chic and very bright, her husband was busy laying his way through the available female population of Cheshire Point. Elly evidently did not realize this. Nan did. She was not entirely sure just what girls had succumbed to his manly charms, but it was pretty obvious that—one—he was cheating on Elly every chance he got, and—two—he got more than a few chances.

Nan had a good memory. She remembered a little scene at a party at Hal and Bev Cooper's, at which time she had had the dubious privilege of watching Ted Carr lead Rita Morgan into an unoccupied bedroom, with one hand on Rita's sashaying rump and the other plunged into her neckline. She remembered the autumn dance at the Cheshire Point Country Club, when Ted and some girl up for the weekend from New York had wandered onto the golf course looking for the nineteenth hole.

Other times, too. Ted was sexy—there was no getting around that; the man positively oozed beddability. And Ted was persistent. He didn't let a girl wonder what he was after.

Right now he was making it obvious.

But only to her. They sat playing bridge, the Haskells against the Carrs, and the game proceeded at its usual pace. Every so often Nan would look up to find Ted Carr's eyes boring very intently into her own. He would smile, slowly, and would go on looking at her until, embarrassed without quite knowing why, she averted her gaze.

Then, when her eyes darted back at him, he would be looking at her again. And that same slow smile would spread on his face.

The smile was not exactly obscene. It came close, however. It said, in a nutshell, I'm Interested In Taking You To Bed And Sooner Or Later I'll Do Just That. And there was something about Ted Carr that didn't let you doubt the idea. If he looked at a woman long enough, and carefully enough, she would melt.

She would permit him to seduce her because she accepted her seduction as inevitable.

Then he started with the foot.

Now, playing footsies is corny. It is corny and square and very definitely Out. If a man starts playing footsies with somebody else's wife, she generally laughs at him.

This was different.

Because Ted somehow managed to do two things. He made the action a burlesque, so that it was funny instead of being corny. And at the same time he let you know that the burlesque itself was just a mask, that he really deep down inside and underneath and from the heart meant every last nudge of it, that he was playing footsies, in short, without being corny about it.

"Two spades," Elly Carr said.

Nan tore her attention back to her cards. She didn't remember the hand, or the bidding, but she had a lousy hand and there was no problem. She passed. Ted raised to four spades, the table passed around, and it was her turn, incredibly, to find an opening lead. She tossed out a singleton diamond and tried to get interested in the play of the hand.

This did not materialize. Ted's foot kept reminding her that he had more on his mind than bridge, and she kept losing track of things, and Elly made the contract with an overtrick, bringing in game and rubber.

It was ridiculous, she thought. She should simply laugh the whole thing off. Exurban males made automatic passes at exurban females; it was part of the game, and the passes were rarely very serious. In Italy men pinch women on busses, not for the sexual thrill and not in an attempt to get the females into bed, but simply as an acknowledgment of their physical attractiveness. In Spain and Latin America, males say complimentary things to passing females. And, in exurbia, men makes passes at other men's wives.

A custom, a form of compliment, symptomatic perhaps of the rather schizoid nature of exurbanite society. Nothing more, certainly.

Oh, yeah?

This, she told herself firmly, was hardly the case. Ted Carr was not a perfunctory pass-tosser. He meant it all. He wanted to take her to bed, and thus he was obviously out of his mind.

How could she possibly be interested? Oh, there had been men before Howard—that was no secret. But there had been no men since Howard and there were not going to be. She was a married woman with children, a happily married woman. She had no intention of tossing a hot little extramarital affair just to relieve the boredom of—

Boredom.

The word stopped her cold. She was bored, she'd been bored all day, she was so damned bored she was ready to go out of her mind. But Christ above, she wasn't bored enough to be a damned fool, wasn't sufficiently staggered by stagnancy to have a highland fling with Ted Carr. Nothing could interest her less. Nothing. Why, she loved Howard, she worshipped him, he was everything she wanted in a husband—

Methinks, a voice said, the lady doth protest too much.

She was troubled. She went on being troubled when Ted went on with his pass-tossing. He made it a little more physical while she was getting a tray ready with coffee and sandwiches after the bridge game was done for the evening. Ted managed to pass through the kitchen on the way to the john, and he managed to be so crude that it was frightening. He came up behind her almost before she knew he was there, slipped an arm around, her, grabbed hold of a breast—

She whirled around.

And he was smiling. "No sense being silly about this," he said, calmly and levelly. "I'm going to get in your pants. I want you and you want it as much as I do."

"I do not!"

"You will."

She felt her temper coming to a boil. "You bastard," she snapped. "I'm in love with Howard!"

"What's love got to do with it?"

She simply stared at him.

"I'm going to lay you," he went on. "And you're going to love it. I'm going to take you on a neat little ride to the moon, Nan-O. And love hasn't got a goddamn thing to do with it. I don't want to love you, Nan-O. I just want to lay you."

And then, infuriatingly, he had touched her breast again. She pushed his hand away and his other hand moved to stroke her below, insinuatingly. The hand was gone in an instant. And Ted Carr was leaving the kitchen, light laughter on his lips.

They drank their coffee, ate their sandwiches. The Carrs left. Nan thought once again that Elly was incredibly unfortunate to be married to such a Grade-A son of a bitch as Ted Carr. And then she banished Ted Carr from her mind for the night.

Not entirely, however.

She and Howard made love that night. They undressed, and

washed up, and brushed their teeth. Nan pulled out the alarm button on the electric clock while Howard got his attaché case in order for the morning's trip to the office. Then, the chores out of the way, they slipped under the covers into each other's arms.

Their lovemaking was slow, gentle, tender. It was the coming together of two very familiar bodies, two bodies which had grown quite used to one another. It was tender, and it was sweet, and it was very meaningful. They moved together, slowly, questingly, and they reached fulfillment together, and they lay close together for several minutes before Howard rolled over to fall asleep.

There was only one thing wrong. It was something that may have been present before in their lovemaking; if so, Nan had never been aware of it in the past. Tonight, though, she was aware of it. The awareness was not at all pleasant, not remotely pleasant. It was, as a matter of fact, thoroughly unpleasant.

Their lovemaking was monotonous.

Not without sparkle, not without drive, not without zest, not without satisfaction.

But without surprise. Totally without surprise.

She knew everything Howard was going to do before he did it. She could lie back and anticipate every caress, every kiss, every stroke and pat and pinch. She could, also, anticipate her own reaction to each caress, her own corresponding and answering caress. The whole affair, from beginning to end, was eminently predictable. It followed the pattern that had already been established in the course of years of marriage.

Thus it was monotonous.

She would not have noticed this if it had not been for Ted Carr. His overtures, majestically subtle at the bridge table and incredibly brazen in the kitchen, had made her acutely aware of sex and its various ramifications. And now, after all that, she and Howard had had sex. And it had been, well, boring.

So now, unwillingly, she thought again of Ted Carr. It would not be love with Ted, as it always was with Howard. It would not be warm. It would not be so thoroughly fulfilling.

But neither would it be so annoyingly predictable!

That was the whole thing. She tried to imagine what it would be like—kissing Ted and being kissed by him, touching him and being touched by him, making love to him. It was ridiculous, she would never do it, nothing could be further from her mind.

And yet—

And yet she *was* thinking about it, *was* wondering. And, to be as painfully truthful as possible, *was* interested.

Damn!

She could not sleep. She had just had sex, and sex almost always brought sleep. But now the very fulfillment of union with Howard left her mysteriously unfulfilled and sleep was not possible. She tossed on her pillows, listening to Howard's measured breathing, remembering again the boring events of the day from the first ringing of the alarm clock through the loneliness up to Howard's return.

Now, suppose she were going to have an affair with Ted. How would they work it? Where would they meet, for the love of God? And what would it be like—what on earth would it be like?

Ridiculous, absolutely absurd, simply ridiculous. She wasn't going to have an affair with Ted. She wasn't going to have an affair with anybody. She was in love with Howard—

Love hasn't got a goddamned thing to do with it. I don't want to love you, Nan-O. I just want to lay you.

Damn!

She took a sleeping pill. After a while, it worked.

CHAPTER 5

Linc Barclay awoke around ten in the morning. He came down to breakfast, buried his face in the *Times,* drank two cups of coffee in stony silence. Then he folded the paper carefully and placed it on the floor beside him. He shook a cigarette loose from a crumpled pack and lighted it, blowing out a thick cloud of smoke.

Roz looked at him across the breakfast table. She saw his high forehead, his deep eyes, his hawk-like nose, his well-trimmed, square-cut black beard. A handsome man. A man she loved.

"Morning," he said.

"*Good* morning?"

He shrugged. "Not especially."

"Hung over?"

He thought that over. "A little bit hung," he admitted. "Nothing drastic, no bombs going off in my skull. Just a quiet to-hell-with-it hangover. It won't kill me."

He had come home for dinner last night, money in his pocket, a bottle of J.W. Dant bourbon on the seat of the car beside him. His agent had come through, after prolonged argument, with five hundred dollars, half of the thousand he had asked for. The banks were closed by the time he got the check, but he had been able to cash it at a check-cashing office on 42nd Street at Sixth

Avenue. They'd eaten dinner, and then Linc had gone to work on the bourbon. Roz drank with him.

"Well," she said now. "Sure you feel okay?"

"Positive."

"What's on today?"

He looked away. "I don't know," he said. "I suppose I should get to work."

"Not if you don't feel—"

"Oh, hell," he said. "Not if I don't feel like writing? I haven't felt like writing for months. I can't sit around waiting until I feel like it. I've got a goddamned book to finish and I have to finish it. We're broke, babe."

"I know."

"And it's such a rotten book." He stubbed out his cigarette, poured a fresh cup of coffee from the Silex. "It's a terrible book. Thirty thousand words done so far and all of them ill-chosen. A stupid plot and a cast of cardboard characters."

"Don't you want to finish it?"

This was familiar ground. They'd had the same conversation for roughly three months now.

"No," he was saying now. "No, I don't want to finish it. But, by Christ, I want it to *be* finished. I want the damn thing out of the way once and for all, and the only way to accomplish that happy end is to grind out another thirty thousand words of drivel to match the thirty thousand words I've got done so far. Jesus, I wish this book were out of the way!"

The book was a mystery, tentatively going under the title of *Murder By Moonlight*. The title would probably be changed, if only because it had a too-familiar ring to it and Linc was certain it had been used before at least once. Now, however, the title was the least of anybody's worries.

"Why don't you try something else?" Roz suggested. "A new book, one you can enjoy working on. Something to break the slump."

"It won't work."

"How do you know?"

"Because I tried. Oh, last week—I didn't bother to tell you about it. I put fresh paper in the typewriter and went to work on a straight novel, just swinging along off the top of my head. I did ten pages."

"Why, that's wonderful!"

"The hell it is. I ripped it up, Roz. It was lousy. Wooden prose, stiff dialogue, the works. Genuinely bad. All I managed to do was waste ten sheets of paper. That's all."

She looked at him, then looked away. "This is a bad one," she said.

"The worst yet."

"It'll straighten itself out, Linc. It—"

"It has to, but God knows how or when. Roz, maybe I should take a job. It wouldn't have to be permanent, just a stop-gap measure until things start to click again. Editorial work, something along those lines. There's no sense starving."

"Is that what you want?"

His hand went to his beard, stroking it thoughtfully. "Sure," he said, forcing a weak grin. "Hell, I can hit one of the cheap houses for a job. I can pick up something that'll mean steady money, a check every week that we can count on. And I'd go on trying to write in the evenings until we worked our way out of this jam, and then—"

"No!"

He looked at her.

"Damn it," she said, "you're a writer, Linc. You're not an editor and you're not a hired hand. You're a writer."

"Some writer."

"Yes, some writer. A damned good writer, Linc. And you don't have to scoot into New York on the damned 8:30 with the rest of the galley slaves. You can stay right here and you can lick this slump. We'll manage."

He reached across the table, rumpling her dark brown hair. "Wise guy," he said. "Tough old broad."

"I mean it, Linc."

"I know you do."

He stood up, stuffing the pack of cigarettes into his shirt pocket, picking up a pack of matches. "What the hell," he said. "I'm going to sit in front of the machine for awhile. The blessed typewriter. Maybe something'll happen. I've been on page 98 of good old *Murder By Moonlight* for one hell of a long time. Maybe I can make it to page 99."

She stayed in her seat and watched him go. She thought how much she loved him, during the good times and the bad times as well. Now he was going to torture himself, was going to tear his hair out trying to make words come, trying to draw water from a dry well. But he had to do this, had to continue going to the typewriter every day and sitting there as long as he could. Eventually something would happen. Eventually the words would come again, the well would yield water, the words would push out at breakneck pace. Then he'd be in his study for hours on end, punching typewriter keys like a madman, going without food and sleep, living on coffee and cigarettes until the book was done and another book was started. When Linc worked, he was a dynamo. Now, in a slump, the current was off and he could do nothing about it.

The slump would end. All slumps ended.

Soon, she wished. God, make it be soon!

CHAPTER 6

Elly Carr hadn't heard the car stop at the curb in front. She was busy vacuuming the living room rug, and the noise of the vacuum cleaner was enough to drown out the sound of the big Buick hardtop pulling to a stop in front of her house. She heard the doorbell, though, and she switched off the vacuum cleaner and glanced out the front window. She saw the Buick, a red and black orgy in chrome, and couldn't place it at first. Who did she know who drove a Buick hardtop? Not one of her friends. Maybe a salesman, maybe—

God, she thought. Maybe a man, tipped off by another man that all you have to do is ring Elly Carr's doorbell and she spreads the welcome mat on her bed for you. Oh, God in heaven!

She went to the door, nervous, upset. But there was no man. Outside was a woman, a very attractive redhead who hid her eyes behind forbidding black glasses.

Maggie Whitcomb.

"Hi," Maggie said. "You busy, Ell?"

"Nope. Come on in. I . . . I didn't recognize the car."

"It's Dave's. I usually take the VW but I felt like a bigger car today. How are you fixed for coffee?"

They sat in the living room and drank black coffee from china cups. Elly hardly knew Maggie Whitcomb, had only spoken to her a half dozen times that she could remember off hand. But in towns like Cheshire Point informality was the rule and open friendliness an obligation. When a community is composed of refugees from New York, all of them tossed together in a place where they have few if any friends, acquaintanceships are made quickly and easily.

"You have a lovely place here," Maggie was saying now. "I've never been over before."

"You should have come sooner." What, Elly wondered, did Maggie Whitcomb want? It seemed strange that she would just drop in for coffee out of the blue. And yet so far it seemed like a purely social call. She wasn't collecting for a charity, wasn't organizing a neighborhood committee, wasn't, in short, doing anything but drinking black coffee and making small talk.

"I suppose you're wondering what prompted this visit, Ell."

"Why—"

Maggie's eyes were twinkling. "You have a perfect right to wonder. It's just that I thought we ought to get to know one another. You seem like the sort of gal I might be able to relax and unwind with. And we've never really had much chance to let down our hair and get acquainted. I mean just the two of us, without a host of drunks around and without Dave and Ted making shop talk all night long."

Dave Whitcomb, Elly remembered, was an assistant producer of a pair of morning TV quiz shows. She tried to remember just what he looked like and couldn't bring his face into mental focus. He was a quiet man, easily dominated in company by his dynamic red-haired wife.

"I'm glad you came," Elly said. "Ted's in the city and Pam's at

school and I've done about as much housework as I feel like doing."

"Then I picked a good time."

"You did." She put down her coffee cup. "How about a sandwich? There's some cold roast in the fridge."

"Oh, I wouldn't want you to bother—"

"It's no bother, Maggie. Just sit here."

She hurried into the kitchen and put sandwiches together,
then brought them back into the living room. They ate slowly,
punctuating their conversation with small talk that was as easy
and relaxed as it was fundamentally irrelevant. Elly found herself
growing more and more at ease. Maggie was a striking woman,
an interesting woman. Maybe, she thought, they would become
close friends. And suddenly she realized just how desperately she
needed a friend.

It sounded corny, but this made it no less true. She had a glut
of friends, a bevy of acquaintances, but there had been something
annoyingly superficial about every relationship she had entered
into since she and Ted had moved to Cheshire Point. There were
friends like Nan Haskell, friends like Rita Morgan and Cynthia
Grass. They were people to talk to, girls to swap recipes with and
otherwise pass time. But no *close* friends, no bosom buddies.

She looked at Maggie now, noticing again how attractive she
was. Lustrous red hair, a full mouth, deep eyes. And a fine figure,
with long shapely legs and high proud breasts. She thought again
of Dave Whitcomb and wondered how come he had managed
to grab off a prize like Maggie. Of course, he made a good living,
and he was supposed to be a sharp guy in his field. But he didn't
have Maggie's verve.

"Pam should be through with school soon," she heard herself say. "I'll have to run over and pick her up."

"Can't she walk home?"

"It's a little far. She's only six."

Maggie nodded. "We don't have children. Sometimes I'm glad of it and sometimes I'm sorry."

"You haven't wanted them?"

"It doesn't really matter whether we want them or not," Maggie said. "Dave is sterile."

"Oh, I'm sorry. I—"

Maggie grinned softly. "Please don't be sorry. Really, it's nothing to be embarrassed about. One summer while he was in college he was in an auto accident, had some back trouble. They took too many x-rays, evidently. And that ended his chances of becoming a father."

"It's permanent?"

"Uh-huh. But it's not that much of a tragedy. Oh, I suppose Dave would like to be a father, but I don't imagine I'm much cut out for motherhood. It's not my line." She smiled again. "But it makes the days lonely, I'll tell you that much."

"You shouldn't let yourself be lonely. Just drop in on me. Any time at all, Maggie."

"You're a doll, Ell. But I hate to make a pest of myself."

"Don't be silly—I like your company."

"And I like you, Ell."

There was something strange about the phrase, something a little funny about the way Maggie's eyes held Elly's, something weird in the intensity of Maggie's gaze. Then Maggie's eyes left hers and studied Elly's body, glancing at breasts and hips. It was almost . . . well, almost *sensual*. A man looking at a woman—

Oh, that was ridiculous. Maggie was looking at her just the way she, in turn, had looked at Maggie. Women did that—they took note of other women's physical attributes. It was a sort of measuring, with no sexual connotations at all.

"I'd better run, Ell. I'll see you soon, won't I?"

"Of course."

"Fine. Thanks for the coffee, and the sandwich. Why don't you drop in on me soon?"

"I will," she promised. "Soon."

She walked Maggie to the door, then went back to the living room and watched the red-haired girl walk down the driveway to the red and black Buick hardtop. She was aware of the fluid grace with which Maggie Whitcomb moved, the way her lush buttocks swayed as she walked, the way her long legs were shaped.

Well, she thought. Now I have a friend.

She lighted a cigarette, sat down on the couch and smoked. Maybe Maggie would make a difference. Maybe if she had a friend she could stop the wild sex, the horrible promiscuity. Maybe Maggie was an answer. Maybe it was loneliness and emotional insecurity that drove her into the arms of men like Rudy Gerber, loneliness and emotional insecurity that made her fantasize about a phantom lover on a sleek black stallion.

Because, she thought, the promiscuity had to stop. Ted was a good husband, a perfect husband. He was faithful to her—she was confident of this—and she certainly had an equal responsibility to be faithful in return. And, if she went on sleeping with any brawny moron who rang her doorbell, Ted would find out. Sooner or later he would learn, and he would be hurt and shocked, and he would leave her.

Poor Ted. She owed him fidelity. And now, with Maggie Whitcomb as a friend, maybe she could mend her ways.

CHAPTER 7

Television is many things to many people. To the great unwashed masses, it is a prime medium of entertainment, a big box which is turned on whenever there is anyone at home to watch it. To a top Hollywood director it was a boon, in that there was finally an entertainment medium which was markedly inferior to motion pictures.

To Dave Whitcomb, television was a way to earn a living. To many Cheshire Point children, television was simply a substitute parent, ready and willing to spend time with them while their biological parents were drinking, dining or fornicating.

To Nan Haskell, television was a bore.

Nan hadn't even wanted to get a set in the first place. She hardly ever watched it, and in Manhattan she and Howard had gotten along perfectly well without a set in the apartment. Now, in Cheshire Point, with two small sons in the house, the television was a permanent fixture. It stood on a TV table in the family room in the basement of their split-level colonial. And now, for the first time in weeks, she was watching it.

Well, not exactly. She had the set turned on, and she was seated in front of it, and her eyes were pointed more or less in the direction of the flickering images on the 24-inch screen. But in another equally valid sense she was not watching television at all.

She did not hear what the fuzzy-headed announcer was saying, and she did not see what was going on upon the screen. She did not know what program she was watching, what channel she was tuned to, or what the hell she was doing in front of the television set, as far as that went. She was killing time, and the television set was on, and that was about all there was to it.

She focused her eyes upon the screen now. The announcer was selling soap, some brand-new washday product which would care for her washing machine and lighten her workday chore load. That, at least, was what the slick announcer was trying to palm off on her. She got to her feet, walked to the set, and flicked a knob that darkened the picture tube and halted the sound.

Then, remembering a picture starring David Niven, she drew back her foot to kick in the picture tube. She stopped just in time, turned on her heel and left the family room.

Everything was such a damned bore. Time was passing her by, time was all over the place and yet she was wasting all the time there was, letting the days sail by without doing anything, without accomplishing anything, without getting any place or doing anything at all.

Bored.

Bored.

Bored—

Read a book, she thought. Read a book, go to a movie, make a dress, hoe the garden, cut the lawn—but she did not want to do these things, had no desire to do these things.

Then what *did* she want?

She knew the answer to that question as well as she knew her own name, as well as she knew that she was bored. What she wanted was a change, a break in the established routine. The introduction of a new element into her life, the element of excitement.

Life had once been exciting. Once she had lived in such a manner that each day was a new adventure, an experiment in dynamic living. But now that period of her life seemed to have come to a sort of end, and that was unfortunate in the extreme. Now she was a wife and mother settled down in a split-level colonial in luxurious exurban Cheshire Point.

And bored to tears.

So, for the tenth or twentieth time that day, she thought of Ted Carr.

She did not think of him in terms of face and body, as a woman might think of a man with whom she was hazily considering the possibility of an extramarital affair. She did not think of him in specifically sexual terms, to be sure, but as a possible means of alleviating all that boredom, of changing all that dreadful monotony.

Great God in heaven, she thought. Now there was a fresh approach—going to bed with somebody else's husband not because you were hot to trot but because you were bored stiff. Getting boffed not for the sheer joy of the boffing but because it might be a change. God!

Well, she thought, just for the sake of argument, what *would* it be like?

In the first place, it would be hidden. It would be something to be carried on in secret, something done on the sly. How? At her home, during the day when Howard and the kids were gone? That would be tough, since Ted had to be in town just as Howard did. In motels? That would be something pretty outré, signing in under an alias in a sleazy motel and stealing a few minutes' worth of lust in a smelly bed. Or maybe, by God, they could do it in the back seat of a car. That would take her back to the days of her youth, all right.

But Ted had a sports car, and it would be difficult. Bucket seats were fine for riding, but—

Well, they could take the Caddy. Plenty of room in the Caddy. Even more room in the station wagon; just toss a mattress on the floor in back and you're ready for action. Then—

Oh, it was ridiculous. The whole thing was insane and she had to forget about it. Had to forget all about it. Had to think about other things like when to pick up Skip and Danny, and what to wear to the PTA meeting, and what to have for dinner, and, well—

Boring.

Boring.

Boring!

She was just about to go to the station wagon and drive down to school to pick up the boys when the phone rang. She hesitated a moment, then went to the phone and lifted the receiver to her ear.

"Hello?"

Silence greeted her. She said hello again, then listened to gentle laughter come over the line.

"Hello yourself," Ted Carr said. "How've you been feeling, Nan-O?"

"What do you want?"

"You."

Just the single word, the second-person-singular pronoun. Just that. It made her gasp.

"You've got your nerve," she said finally. "You've really got a hell of a lot of nerve, calling me like this."

"Busy, Nan-O?"

"Damn it—"

"I just thought you might have been doing a little thinking, Nan-O. About our discussion last night."

"Ted—"

"Because I still think we might have a ball," he went on. "You've got beautiful breasts, Nan-O. I'd like to touch them. Kiss them, play with them. I want to get in your pants, Nan-O."

She hated him. And yet his words were reaching her, getting to her. She squirmed uncomfortably, passion beginning to mount up unwillingly in her system.

"Hot, Nan-O. All hot and ready to go?"

"Ted—"

"Let me draw you a picture," he went on. "You'll be lying on a bed. You'll have your skirt way up over your waist and your panties down around your knees. And I'll be working you up, getting you so hot you can't stand it. You'll beg for it, Nan-O. You'll crawl to me on your dimpled knees. And then—"

"*Stop it!*"

A wicked laugh. "I'll ring off now, Nan-O. But think it over. I'll call again soon."

He hung up before she could answer him. Think about it? She shuddered.

She could think of nothing else.

CHAPTER 8

Dave Whitcomb took Maggie out to dinner that night.

This was not unexpected. It was a Wednesday night, and Dave always took Maggie out to dinner on Wednesday, before heading over to the weekly poker game at Len Barnes' house. They went, as always, to The Gables, an old Cheshire Point mansion which had been converted into an Early American style restaurant. They had a pair of extra-dry martinis to start, a pair of shrimp cocktails, a pair of chef's salads with Roquefort. Maggie ordered the roast beef while Dave had a blood-rare strip sirloin. Dave talked about how the shows had gone that morning, and Maggie mentioned her visit to Elly Carr.

The dinner was not exciting. Dave and Maggie did not have an especially exciting marriage, yet it was for each the most desirable solution to their own personal problems. The Whitcombs, man and wife, were united far less by love than by an affectionate tolerance. Each was a support for the other, a help for the other.

Maggie had lied to Elly Carr. Dave Whitcomb was not sterile. He and Maggie had never had any children not because Dave had spent too much time in front of an x-ray machine but because he and Maggie had never made love. They were in their seventh year of marriage, were very happy together, and could not conceivably regard divorce as even a remote possibility. Yet they slept in separate beds, and stayed in their respective beds, and never exchanged more than a public kiss.

There was a reason for this.

Dave was a homosexual, and Maggie was a lesbian.

To look at them, of course, you could never have guessed this cheerful little fact. Dave could hardly have looked less like the popularized concept of the homosexual. He wore his hair in a mud-brown crew-cut, didn't swish when he walked, and wore standard latter-day Ivy League clothing, maybe a shade quieter than most of his Cheshire Point friends. He never minced, never lisped, and seemed on the surface to be one-hundred percent heterosexual.

Like the majority of American homosexuals, Dave worked very hard to keep his sex life and his business and social life as far separated as possible. His poker friends were heterosexual, his business acquaintances were also heterosexuals; as a matter of full fact, he was a homosexual with absolutely no homosexual friends. Once or twice a week, when he wanted to meet a lover, he would go to any of several homosexual bars in New York, either in Greenwich Village or around the intersection of 72nd Street and Broadway. There he would meet someone, proceed to the other man's apartment or to a hotel room, and have sexual relations. He was always careful never to permit his lover to learn his real name or address. He was an up-and-coming man in the television industry, a rising star in the production end; public knowledge of his sexual tastes could not possibly do him any good.

Sometimes, when he had little time to fence around or when his usual haunts failed to turn up a prospect, he would go to a male prostitute. He would meet any of a number of overgrown effeminate juvenile delinquents at a cafeteria on the north side of 42nd Street at Times Square, and for anywhere from five to thirty dollars he would enjoy the young man's favors. He didn't like to do this. It was sordid, for one thing; for another, he risked a beating or a robbery. But there were times when he had no choice.

On the surface, Dave Whitcomb's life was eminently normal, eminently respectable. A happily married man with a beautiful wife and a good position in a dynamic industry.

If Dave did not fit the public image of the homosexual, Maggie in turn could not have less resembled the stereotyped lesbian. Her hair was long, not butch-cut. Her dress was feminine and in perfect taste. She used quite a bit of makeup. She looked, as one male country club member had remarked to another in a wistful voice, as though she might be a joyful nymphomaniac. Every pore of Maggie seemed to ooze sex. The sex, however, was directed solely at other women.

The Whitcombs finished dinner. Dave paid the check, left a large tip, and led the way to the Buick, which was parked in The Gables' parking lot. He put a quarter into the attendant's hand, opened the door for Maggie, closed it, walked around the car, opened his door, got behind the wheel, fitted the key into ignition, turned the key, stepped on the gas pedal, and drove off.

"Well," he said finally. "So you're putting on the make for little Elly Carr."

"I didn't say that."

"You don't have to," he said. "Not in so many words. Be careful as hell, Mag."

"I'm a careful person."

"I'm not kidding," he went on. "All you have to do is tip your hand before she's ready to play ball and we've had it. The odds are about eighty-three to one that she'll tell all the world just how gay you are. You know what that would mean?"

"Leaving Cheshire Point, I suppose."

"Leaving the country," he said, "would be more like it. We'd be in a pretty little spot. I frankly wish you'd stick to New York lesbians instead of trying to make converts. There's a maxim—Don't crap where you eat."

"You don't have to worry."

"Don't I?"

"No," Maggie said. "I can be very subtle, David."

"You'll have to be."

"Very subtle. Elly will be the one who thinks *she's* dragging *me* to bed, not the other way around. You want to know something? I think she's one of those gals who's gay without knowing it. I was cruising her gently today, giving her big eyes without being obvious about it. She didn't figure out what I was doing, but I think I was reaching her. It shouldn't be hard to let her wind up in bed with me."

"Just be very careful, Mag."

She told him again not to worry, that she would be tremendously careful. Then they were at their home, a streamlined ranch decorated in perfect modern taste by a homosexual interior decorator who managed to spend two weeks with Mag and Dave without guessing that they were gay. She stepped out of the car, stood for a moment on the sidewalk while the big Buick hardtop pulled away from the curb, then turned and headed up the walk to the front door.

The night was cool, clear. The air had a crisp edge to it and she waited for a few seconds, her key in the lock, filling her lungs with fresh air and letting herself unwind. Then she turned the key, pushed open the door and went inside.

She made herself a drink, putting one large ice cube in a high-ball glass and covering it with a lot of Scotch and a splash of soda. She sat down with her drink on the long low couch and thought about Elly Carr.

Elly, she thought, was not going to be anywhere near as easy as she had made her sound to Dave. You had to make sex a simple matter for David, because his own attitude toward sexual activity was, in essence, a simple one. Love never entered into his concept of the overall scheme of things, and a permanent or semi-permanent relationship with a homosexual partner was something he could not possibly desire. He was fully satisfied with hit-and-run sex, in which his partner did not know his name and the two of them were together only long enough to arrive at their desperate little orgasms.

She was not built that way. Anonymous pick-ups and quickie affairs were not her dish of tea, and that was all there was to it. She had tried them—she remembered all too vividly the evening when Rhonda Michaels, her love-of-the-moment, had failed to put in an appearance at the Partial Dome on Cornelia Street. So, oversexed and overtired, she had permitted a butchy type named Jo to pick her up. Jo had small breasts and broad shoulders and a deep voice, and she swore like an unhappy truck driver. She took Maggie to a filthy apartment on the Lower East Side, filled her with rotgut wine, peeled off her clothes, played with her breasts, and spent about two hours kissing her. She had never seen Jo again. And, if she never did, that was fine.

From a purely physical standpoint, the experience with Jo had been satisfying enough. She'd been extremely excited, and she'd reached orgasm, and that much was fine. But it was sex in a vacuum, meaningless and pointless sex that made Maggie Whitcomb feel cheap and dirty inside. When you were thirsty you drank a glass of water; when you were itchy you picked up someone else who was itchy and you went to bed. That was Dave's philosophy and Jo's philosophy as well. It did not work for Maggie.

She needed love, or some reasonable facsimile thereof. She needed affection and understanding and a genuine emotional attachment. She needed a relationship that exceeded the bounds of the bed, a relationship that satisfied more urges than the purely pubic ones. She did not need, or want, a genuinely enduring relationship, a genuinely sincere love. She did not need or want anything that would make her want to leave Dave Whitcomb or anything that would make her live a gay life instead of the one she lived now, complete with its veneer of heterosexuality. More than one affair had ended because her partner had demanded more than Maggie had been willing to give.

She sighed. She sipped her drink, which was a little stronger than she liked it. She lighted a cigarette, smoked, put the cigarette out. She finished her drink, set the empty glass upon an end table, and stretched out on her back upon the couch. For a few minutes her eyes stared sightlessly at the ceiling. Then they were closed.

She thought, again, about Elly Carr.

Elly was very lovely. That was the first thing—Elly was beautiful, and Maggie couldn't help thinking of her in sexual terms, imagining herself cupping Elly's girlish breasts in her own trembling hands, imagining Elly's mouth kissing her and Elly's hands stroking her body in return. In her mind she could taste Elly's mouth, could sense the thrilling contact of Elly's bare flesh against her own. Elly's legs all tangled up with her own legs, Elly's body pressed tight against her own. Elly, Elly Elly Elly—

She had never before attempted to seduce a woman in Cheshire Point. The arguments Dave had advanced were not ones which had not already occurred to her a thousand times, arguments which flooded into her mind every time she felt herself attracted to a woman in the exurbanite community. But this time she was not going to repress her desires. They were too strong. A lover in Greenwich Village could not dissipate her insatiable ache to get Elly on a bed.

And it was not as though she would be breaking up an ideal marriage. She was hardly the home wrecker type, and she had no intention of taking Elly away from her husband. Elly would go on being married to Ted Carr, and Maggie would seduce her and they would have their fling, and in time Elly would be back in Ted's arms and none the worse for wear.

And Ted Carr had no right to expect fidelity from his wife. That was another point, and a pretty damned valid one. Ted Carr would and did go for anything in a skirt. He had tried, more than once, to go for Maggie. Not knowing that she was a lesbian, and firmly convinced that he was Christ's gift to American womanhood, and strongly attracted by her breasts and hips and all-around sexuality, he had made his passes. It had been, if nothing else, a little awkward.

She had solved it neatly. She had told him, gently but firmly, that if he bothered her again with his sexual suggestions she would cut off his manhood.

This worked. He had turned a rather attractive shade of green and had stalked off, never to offer his fair white body to her again. An emasculated Ted Carr would be like an unarmed gunman or a defrocked priest, and the thought alone was enough to put him off permanently.

Ted Carr, though, was a louse.

That was the whole point. He was a louse, and he was cheating right and left on Elly, and what was sauce for the gander was undeniably sauce for the goose as well. Which was why the thought of introducing Elly Carr to the highways and byways of female homosexuality did not exactly strike Maggie as patently immoral.

Her eyes were still closed. She was thinking back now, thinking all the way back to the first time. It had been years ago, many years ago. It had happened at her high school, a fancy girls' boarding school in New England where only girls from the better families were accepted.

And, she thought, where more subjects were offered than were listed in the school catalogue.

Her first two years had been virtually sexless. The very few dates with boys had done nothing to her virginal status. She was sixteen, in her junior year, before sex reared its lovely head in the majestic person of a girl named Lily Raines.

Lily was tall and slender, a senior girl with a shock of jet black hair and the hollowest, deepest eyes Maggie had ever seen. Maggie was working on the school yearbook, which Lily Raines edited, and they became friendly. That was the beginning.

The friendship ripened. They talked about everything, were together constantly. They discussed sex and love and life. They sipped wine behind closed doors.

And one night it went a little further than that.

They were in Lily's room. The dark-haired girl put a stack of records on, mood music with muted horns and a few thousand violins. "Let's dance," she suggested. "I haven't danced with anyone in ages."

They danced. They had been drinking red wine and it had gone to Maggie's head. She was a little dizzy and a little sleepy. She moved with the music, close against Lily, and something began to happen.

She felt Lily's breasts pressing against her own breasts, felt Lily's hands rubbing her back and shoulders. She pushed tighter against Lily, inhaling her sweet perfume, smelling her and touching her, and, all at once, *needing* her.

Then Lily kissed her. The room rocked, and reason fell out the window, and things began to happen in a cosmic realm away from space and time. Lily handled her breasts, coaxing the rosebud nipples into new awareness, making them swell with passion. Lily kissed the tips of those breasts, ran her tongue around each nipple in tantalizing circles.

The night was long.

And now Maggie Whitcomb was a lesbian. Now she lay on a couch in a ranch house, eyes closed, breathing shallow. She was thinking about Elly Carr. She was going to make Elly feel the way Lily had made *her* feel, was going to do to Elly all the wonderful and mystic things that Lily had so capably taught her.

She smiled.

Chapter 9

Roz Barclay didn't have to ask the question.

There were times when you did not have to ask certain questions. When your husband walked in the side door with his shoulders slumped, with his beard drooping and his eyes vacant, you did not ask him how it had gone at the sweet old typewriter. You knew damned well that it had gone horribly, so there was very little point in asking.

Even so, she said: "A bad day?"

He nodded.

"Nothing?"

"Nothing at all. A page, one goddamned page to show for six goddamned hours staring at the keyboard of the goddamned typewriter. It's not even a good page, Roz. I'll look at it in the morning and tear it to ribbons. It's a lousy page."

"It's one less page to write."

"Not if I tear it up." He shrugged. "Oh, hell. Maybe I'll write another one tomorrow. At that rate it'll take three months to finish the lousy book. Unless I shoot myself first."

She thought it might be a good time to change the subject. "Hungry? I can fix you something to eat."

"You have dinner already?"

"I took a sandwich. I didn't want to interrupt you. What can I get you?"

"Nothing," he said.

"Positive?"

"Positive. I'm not hungry. Let's make love, Roz."

Her heart quickened. "Do you . . . do you want to?

"I'd love to."

She went to him, her eyes shining, her heart full of love for him. She pressed close to him, looking up into his face, hoping that it would happen, that they would be able to make love, that her body could bring him satisfaction and permit him to relax and come out of his shell.

"Come on," she said. "Let's go upstairs."

They went upstairs. Her heart stayed full of hope, an almost desperate hope. She needed him. They went into the bedroom, closed the door. She went into his arms and their mouths met in a kiss. She gripped him tight, held onto him, clinging to him like a barnacle to the side of an ocean liner. Her tongue stabbed into his mouth and her hips ground against his with verve which a burlesque dancer would have been proud of and which a prostitute would have envied.

They undressed quickly. They stood nude and kissed, and her blood began to pound through veins and arteries. She felt his hairy chest against her bare breasts, felt his hands stroking her back and backside. She needed him with a blind and aching need.

It had to work. It had to—she needed him and he needed her and it had to work now, had to break right for him. Maybe one could cure the other, maybe if they made love it would shake the slump loose, maybe sex could release creative energy and he could get back to work on the book.

She was not certain. She knew now only that she needed him, that it had to work.

Period.

They groped their way to the bed. He tore off the blankets and they stretched out on the bed, their bodies together, their arms around each other. His tongue stabbed into her mouth and his hands were on her breasts, holding them, squeezing them. He was hurting her and the pain was a delight to her, an ache that was delicious. He squeezed once more and she writhed in passion.

"I love you, Roz—"

"Linc—"

"I love you, Roz baby. Oh, Christ, I love you. I love you so damned much."

"God, Linc—"

"So beautiful. Such beautiful breasts. You could make a fortune with them. Roz. You could model with them for paperback covers."

"Kiss them, Linc—"

He did not need to be coaxed. He moved lower on the bed and his lips found the valley between the two breasts. Her skin was very soft there, very sensitive, and his tongue reached out to tease the tender skin. She squirmed, needing him, and he kissed her, moving from the valley to the mountains themselves.

He kissed first one breast and then the other. She was alive with lust now, alive with need, and she put her hands on the back of his head and pressed his face into her breasts, loving the tricks he performed so perfectly with lips and tongue.

His hands dropped to her thighs. He squeezed her and a tiny moan escaped her lips.

"Linc—"

His hands were clever. God, how she needed him! She loved him and needed him and she had to have him or die.

"Linc—"

And then suddenly, too suddenly, he was moving away from her. His eyes were pools of terror and his face was white. His shoulders sagged and his chin fell.

"What's the matter?"

"I can't," he snapped. "I can't, that's all. That's what's the goddamned matter."

"Oh, darling—"

"I'm a first class son of a bitch," he said. "I managed to get you all worked up and now I can't finish the job. I don't know what the hell is wrong with me, honey. Maybe I ought to go blow my brains out. Maybe that's the answer."

"Don't talk like that!"

He shrugged, impatient with himself. "I'm a son of a bitch," he said again. "I didn't think this could happen, Roz. I . . . I really wanted you. I needed you. I thought it would work."

"I understand."

"I thought it would work, that everything would be all right, that I would be able to. It didn't work."

"You're all tied up in knots," she said. "You're in a stinking slump and it's a vicious circle. It's nothing to worry about."

"No?"

"No, Linc. It's all right."

He turned away. "Look," he said, "I have to get out of the house, have to be by myself for awhile."

"I understand."

"I'm going into town," he said. "I'll head over to the tavern, have a few drinks. I've got to straighten myself out."

"All right."

"Don't wait up for me."

She waited in bed while he dressed, left the bedroom. She listened for the slam of the door, then heard him start the car's engine and drive off into the night. She hoped he'd be all right—he had a tendency to drink too much when he was depressed, and he was about as depressed now as she had ever seen him.

But he held his liquor well. He would be home all right. She did not have to worry about him.

She lay for a few minutes in the darkness.

Alone, she cried.

CHAPTER 10

Thursday and Friday were ordinary days in Cheshire Point, ordinary days with ordinary weather and ordinary turns of events. Linc Barclay, who had come home drunk as a skunk when the bar closed Thursday morning, spent all of Thursday trying to get over a hangover and all day Friday trying to write. He managed the first, thanks to a liberal quantity of black coffee and several B-complex vitamin pills. The second was still impossible. Two pages—bad ones, he assured Roz—rolled through the typewriter in the course of a nine-hour stint on Friday. That was all.

Thursday afternoon a salesman came to Elly Carr's house. He was a college kid, working his way through school by selling sets of encyclopedias to people who did not really want sets of encyclopedias at all. Elly Carr did not want what he was selling. But, when she looked at the muscular young man, she did want something. She wanted him.

"It was one for the books," he told a friend that night, sitting over glasses of draft beer in a saloon in Brooklyn, where he lived. "She was a cute little number. She came to the door all dolled up in tight slacks and a tighter sweater. She let me get my foot in the door, then invited me inside. We sat down in the living room. I started to go into my routine, telling her just how much her lousy family needed a lousy *Global Encyclopedia and World Atlas*. But I didn't get very far.

"First she brought me a cup of coffee and a sandwich. Then she suggested we sit together on the couch so she could hear me better. And the next thing I knew she was fumbling with my shirt, and her hand was on my chest, see? I was going out of my skull. I didn't get it, you know. I thought it was happening to somebody else, see? I was dreaming it, or something.

"So I just let her alone. And she went on with what she was doing, and she started talking to me, talking dirty. You wouldn't believe the filthy words that came out of that little rosebud mouth. She had me climbing the lousy walls, fooling around with me like that and talking like that.

"I grabbed onto her boobs and we started making out like madmen. It didn't take her long to show me the way to that bedroom of hers. She took off her goddamned clothes and stood there like a marble statue, you know, and I just touched everything in sight. She was the hottest thing going, man. Hot as a Roman candle.

"And we made it. It was . . . Jesus, I don't know. She knew more tricks than any broad I ever got close to in my life. She was . . . great, that's all. We wound up on the moon. Then she told me to get to hell out, so I put on my pants and went home.

"I figured that was enough work for the day. I just didn't feel like peddling the goddamned *Global Encyclopedia and World Atlas* any more. Man, you never met a woman like that! Imagine being married to her, for God's sake—her poor husband must carry his scrotum around in a wheelbarrow. I bet she drives him nuts."

The college kid didn't know that Elly lay in bed crying after he left. She was horribly depressed. After the Rudy Gerber affair, and after Maggie Whitcomb's visit had suggested that a friendship with Maggie might prove a solution to her promiscuity, she had taken a very solemn vow not to make love with anyone but Ted.

And now—

Now she had broken that vow. Now a broad-shouldered college kid had come stumbling in the door with some crud about an encyclopedia, and she had practically raped the little idiot. Phantom lover—oh, it was all such a mess, such a goddamn mess!

Elly had planned on going to Maggie's that afternoon. She'd wanted to talk to her, to get to know her better. But now she couldn't bring herself to see anyone. She felt filthy, inside and out, filthy and rotten and crawling and disgusting. The shower she took did not help, and when she changed the bed linen, as she always did after an act of infidelity, it seemed like a vacuous gesture, a sickening attempt to erase the immensely wrong act she had been so responsible for.

She did not go to Maggie's. She stayed home that day, sitting around, glancing through a magazine, letting time pass.

Friday, in the afternoon, she dropped in on Maggie Whitcomb.

Thursday and Friday were dull days for Nan Haskell, but this did not surprise her. It seemed now as though every day was a dull day, as though every day would go on being a dull day until, one dull day, her heart stopped beating and she died. On Thursday morning and on Friday morning as well she awoke at fourteen minutes to seven when the electric alarm clock screamed its message of wakefulness into her ears. She brushed her teeth, washed her face, made Howard's breakfast, drove him to the station. She returned each morning to wake the boys, to feed them, to run them down to their school. Then her own breakfast, and the house cleaning, and the shopping and what a damned bore it all was!

Then a call from Ted.

Thursday, at two in the afternoon, she was angry that he had called. This time his call was a little stronger—he used vulgar words, and extraordinarily descriptive phrases, and he told her just what he was going to do with her and just what she was going to do with him and just how much they would both enjoy it. The words had a bizarre effect upon her. She wanted to hang up on him but somehow she could not. The receiver stayed glued to her ear, and her hands began trembling involuntarily, and she listened to every obscene word and felt her heartbeat quicken in response.

She welcomed his call on Friday. She waited for it, like a teenage girl waiting for her steady boy friend to call her away from her homework, and when the phone rang she ran to answer it. He said hello, his voice husky, and she answered him warmly.

He laughed.

"You're getting interested," he said. "Aren't you, Nan-O?"

She didn't answer.

"You want me," he went on confidently. "You were all cold and angry at first, but you've been thinking it over, and now your mind is changing. You want Ted between your legs, Nan-O. Don't you?"

"Maybe I do."

Her words surprised her. She had not meant to say them, had not even meant to think them, but they had come from her lips against her will. There was no way to call them back now. They had been said, and he had chuckled warmly in response, and the die seemed to have been cast.

"When, Nan-O?"

She swallowed.

"When?"

"I don't want to talk about it."

"Neither do I," he said levelly. "I want to do it. Doing is more fun than talking, Nan-O."

"Ted—"

"Not over the weekend," he said. "I think I'll spend the weekend with wife and child. Next week, Nan-O. Monday or Tuesday, say. How does that sound to you, Nan-O?"

"I don't know."

"Think about it," he said, his voice dripping lust. "Dream about it, Nan-O. Monday or Tuesday. It's a date."

About the time Nan Haskell was replacing the receiver on the hook with shaking hands, Elly Carr was drinking black coffee laced with Scotch at Maggie Whitcomb's house.

"It's a little wicked, I suppose," Maggie had said. "But hell, Ell. We girls lead a strenuous life. A wee drink in the afternoon never hurt anybody, did it?"

"Never," Elly had agreed.

"Besides, it's solitary drinking that's bad. And we're drinking together. That makes it social drinking, and it's in coffee anyway, and what the hell. Cigarette, Ell?"

She had taken the cigarette, had sipped the coffee. Now the cigarette was butted dead in a wide copper ashtray and the coffee cup was half-empty. Maggie was right, she had to admit. A little drink in the middle of the afternoon was hardly harmful, and it did do wonders to relax a person. Maybe that was what she needed—maybe, if she took a drink instead of a door-to-door salesman, she could get the same effect without being a round-heeled little tramp.

Of course there were dangers in that course of action. Every suburb and exurb had its quota of female alcoholics, lonely wives who searched for companionship in the bottom of bottles. Cheshire Point could boast of half a dozen women in that leaky canoe, and Elly didn't want to wind up sharing their boat without a paddle.

But all this was ridiculous. She was only visiting a friend and drinking a cup of Irish coffee—or did you call it Scotch coffee when you used Scotch instead of Irish whisky? Well, whatever you called it, that was all she was doing. And for her to worry about alcoholism was about as nutty as you could get. She had better things to worry about, things like that encyclopedia-peddling college boy, things like Rudy Gerber, things like all the men who came to her door and wound up in her bed.

That sort of thing.

"What we both need," Maggie was saying, "is a shopping trip. We could take a late train into New York, right after you get Pam on her way to school and spend the day on Fifth Avenue. We'd be back in time for you to pick up your darling daughter and get home to cook dinner."

"Or Pam could go over to a friend's house after school. That would save an hour or two."

"It's what we both need," Maggie said. "How long has it been since you went into the city to shop?"

"Too long. I usually shop at Alexander's, the upper Westchester branch. It's convenient."

"Very convenient."

"Very convenient. But somehow Alexander's isn't the same as Fifth Avenue, Ell."

"Cheshire Point isn't the same as Manhattan."

Maggie smiled. "You just said a mouthful. I miss New York, Ell. The air is better and the country is healthy as hell, and a house is more fun than an apartment, but I miss New York."

"I do, too. I was born there."

"Let's go, then. On Monday. We'll spend our husbands into the poorhouse and have lunch at the top of the Tishman Building and have an all-around ball. Is it a date?"

"It's a date," Elly said.

"More coffee? Your cup's empty."

"It must have a hole in it. Easy on the Scotch, huh?"

"Sure."

They were midway through their second cups of coffee when Maggie raised her arms over her head and stretched, her breasts jutting out against the thin white cloth of her blouse. "I don't know about you," she said, "but I think it's hot as hell in here."

"It is a little warm."

"I'd turn on the air-conditioner, except there isn't one. If I were alone I'd take my blouse off."

"Well, go ahead."

Maggie grinned. "Sure you don't mind? After all, it's just us girls here. But I don't want to behave like an exhibitionist."

"Go ahead," Elly said. "I don't mind."

She tried not to look at Maggie as the red-haired girl

unbuttoned her white blouse and drew it back over her shoulders. But something forced her to watch. She was vaguely uncomfortable without knowing quite why. Maggie took off the blouse and set it beside her on the long low couch. Her bra was black and lacy, and she looked down at it and giggled softly.

"My one gross affectation," she said. "I have a weakness for sexy underwear. I'm wearing a pair of peekaboo panties, believe it or not. Sexy as hell."

Elly wanted to look away. She couldn't. Maggie, she noticed, had perfect breasts, much larger than her own but firm with no tendency to sag or droop. And the black lacy bra *was* sexy; there was no question about it. But, as Maggie had said, it was just us girls here. Why should she react to Maggie's near-nudity?

"That's more like it, Ell. I'd take the bra off too, but this isn't a strip show, is it? God, it's nice to get air on my skin. Why don't you pull that sweater over your head and relax?"

"Well—"

"Go on. It's ten degrees cooler, woman. Try it."

Why not, she thought. She pulled her yellow sweater up over her head and put it beside her on the chair. Only then did she remember that she had not taken the trouble to wear a bra. She blushed a deep red.

"Well," Maggie said. "I guess this *is* a strip show."

"I'm . . . I'm sorry."

"It's nothing to be sorry about, sweetie."

"I just forget to bother with a bra some of the time."

"I can see why. You don't need one. You've got a knockout figure, Elly."

"Thank you." Why did the compliment make her feel funny?

She was being silly today. Maybe it was the Scotch in the coffee; she wasn't used to drinking in the afternoon.

"If you can wave your breasts around," Maggie went on, "I won't bother with false modesty. I'll take my bra off and relax."

She slipped her hand around her back, struggled with the catch on the brassiere. "Damn," she said. "Give me a hand, will you, sweetie? I'm all thumbs today."

A little shaky, she went to Maggie and opened her bra for her. Her hands were moist with perspiration, and she shivered slightly when her fingers brushed the silky skin of Maggie's back. But Maggie didn't appear to notice. She thanked her, took off the bra, and set it aside.

"Now," she said, "we are a pair of nudists. Fun?"

"Fun," Ellie agreed. And her eyes went automatically to Maggie's breasts. They were beautiful, simply beautiful. Very large, very creamy, with ruby tips for nipples. But why on earth should she want to look at another girl's breasts? She had breasts of her own, even if they weren't as large as Maggie's. She could just look in the mirror if she wanted.

"You're lovely," Maggie said. "Ted's a lucky guy."

Sure, she thought. Lucky he's got a cheating wife.

"You're not bad yourself," she answered. "Dave's fairly fortunate himself."

"Do you really think so?"

"Of course."

Maggie smiled gently. "You're sweet, Ell. You're sweet."

Elly left in time to pick up Pam at school. She felt moderately light-headed from the Scotch, but hardly under the influence. And, back under her own roof, she felt faintly disturbed about her own reactions to Maggie's bare breasts. God, she didn't have the hots for Maggie now, did she? That would be just a little too much. It was bad enough to lay for every man in the area without making passes at women, for the love of God. She might be a nymphomaniac, but she sure as shooting was not a lesbian to boot.

She laughed at herself. She was being silly now. Maggie was a friend, a very good friend, and she certainly had no sexual designs on the poor girl. Monday they would go into New York on a shopping spree, and they would have a good time, and their friendship would grow.

She looked forward to Monday.

CHAPTER 11

As Howard Haskell had once remarked to Nan, the best thing about Cheshire Point was that you only spent a limited amount of time there during the day. He was thinking from the male point of view, of course, and he was discounting the weekends. On Saturday and Sunday, the ad men and PR men and television men of Cheshire Point let the 8:03 cannonball into Grand Central without them. They had the weekend to spend with families and friends at leisure.

It was hell.

There is no point in examining this particular weekend in Cheshire Point under a microscope, or even through a pair of high-powered binoculars. It was a very normal every-week weekend at the Point, which is to say that it was slightly less than bearable for all concerned. The natives of the Point, free from their New York jobs and the commuting rat-race for two days, were hell-bent upon proving to themselves that living in the country was relaxed and happy and, above all, fun.

There were parties, dozens of them, and every family managed to go to one party Friday night and another on Saturday night. The parties were alcoholic, with gallons of booze going down throat after scarified throat. Men flirted half-seriously with the other men's wives, drank themselves sick, weaved their cars home and passed out. Children watched late movies on television while teenaged boys kissed or necked or petted with or had intercourse with their baby sitters, town girls paid the outrageous sum of one dollar per hour in return for raiding the refrigerator, messing up the living room and entertaining their boy friend in comparative privacy.

The less said about the weekend, the better.

It was a weekend in Cheshire Point. That, really, is the essence of it. It was a weekend in Cheshire Point, with weekend guests being introduced to the delights of life in the country, with liquor flowing and tempers unwinding and sex periodically rearing its lovely head. Little of real interest transpired. Perhaps a few isolated events might give you an idea what it was like.

At one party, a very well established songwriter went to the piano and played and sang Cole Porter's "You're The Top." The melody, sung off-tune as it was, was still Porter's. The lyrics were this particular Cheshire Point songwriter's own, and they were obscene. The first line ran *You're the top, you're the mound of Venus,* and the song moved onward and upward from that point, reaching delirious heights.

For awhile, the audience laughed. Then the audience began to get a bit worried. Then the songwriter stood up shakily, staggered away from the piano, and grabbed the first woman he saw. He took hold of her by her big breasts, kissing her passionately, and propositioned her in words substantially the same as those he had used in his parody of the Cole Porter tune.

The woman happened to be his own wife. This fact eased the tension in the room, and no one really minded when the songwriter and his wife hurried off to a convenient bedroom to ease the pangs of sexual abstinence. But the songwriter had not realized that the woman he selected was his wife. The possibility never occurred to him. He took her to bed, made love to her, and rolled off sleepily.

"God," he said to her, his eyes shut tight. "God, my wife'll kill me when she hears about this. But you're worth it, baby. You're the best I ever had."

His wife, basking in the afterglow of inspired sex, did not hit the roof. After all, she had just been complimented, albeit in a left-handed fashion. Besides, her husband earned forty-five thousand dollars a year. Husbands like that were hard to find.

She dressed quickly and let him sleep it off. She did not want him to find out, when he awoke, that his great adventure had been with his own wife.

It would be better to let him feel guilty.

That example should give you the general idea. Or take the case of another woman, a senior editor at a respected hardcover publishing house who was married to a mousy little partner in a third-rate advertising agency. This woman worked under enormous pressure, staying late in New York three nights out of five. When the weekend came, she let herself go. She drank.

She started drinking Friday evening, in the club car on the way home from the office. She went on drinking through dinner, and then she and her husband went to a party where the liquor flowed freely. In no time at all she was feeling no pain.

She behaved herself that Friday night. But Saturday, when she awoke, she was thrilled to discover that the hangover she had every right to expect had not yet arrived. The alcohol was still circulating in her bloodstream, and instead of being hung over she was still drunk.

She had no intention of letting such a head start go to waste. She went downstairs wrapped up in a nightgown, found a bottle of gin, and made martinis for breakfast.

She kept drinking all day long, never going over the edge but always staying on the drunk side of the spectrum.

That evening, at a party, she went over the edge.

She did a great many things, most of which should be mercifully forgotten. She found magnificently vile things to say to a wide variety of people, including her host and hostess. She danced obscenely on a table top, screamed at the top of her lungs, broke out into horrible fits of crying and then began laughing hysterically. Her meek and mild-mannered husband finally led her out of the house after she climaxed things by leaping gaily onto the dining room table, hoisting her skirt over her head and soiling the punch bowl. This was a little too much, even on a weekend in Cheshire Point.

CHAPTER 12

The weekend.

Roz Barclay was home, alone. Linc had gone down to the tavern. She knew that he would not be there long, that he would not get particularly drunk. She knew, too, that she was home alone, that she was bored, that she was frustrated, and that she was about to go out of her mind.

She took a deep breath.

Other women, she thought, had it easier. More than a few Cheshire Point women had more than one man on tap—Roz knew this for a fact. She knew it about the ones who damn near advertised. She'd seen Harry Barnes, the plumber, go into Mindy Pierce's house at least twice a week for the past two months, never staying less than an hour and always leaving with a smile of animal satisfaction on his fat face. Now the plumbing in an older home may well require the services of a plumber once a month. But the Pierces had a spanking new ranch home, less than three years old, and they surely didn't need Harry Barnes in a professional capacity.

Mindy Pierce, however, evidently needed Harry in a bedroom capacity. And made no bones about it, since it was fairly obvious by now to the whole town. The women talked about it and the men shared knowing looks. Roz didn't talk about it, except for the usual wife-to-husband talks she had with Linc, because she felt that what Mindy Pierce did in her bedroom was none of Roz Barclay's business.

Roz found a pack of cigarettes, shook one loose and lit it. She smoked slowly, thoughtfully. It wasn't as though Mindy Pierce, raven-haired and sharp-eyed and large-breasted, was the only Cheshire Point housewife who had mattress matinees. There were others. Roz, quiet and thoughtful, knew a lot of dirt about a lot of people. She didn't gossip, didn't spread bad news far and wide. She didn't even keep her eyes open. But it was easy to know what was going on.

Easy to know, for example, that Ted Carr was God's gift to Cheshire Point womanhood, self-proclaimed and self-acknowledged as such. Ted slept with any woman handy, and the women of Cheshire Point were most noticeably handy in this respect.

But everybody knew about Ted Carr.

Roz also knew about Elly Carr. This, as it happened, was a deep dark secret. It was a magnificent secret—Ted Carr, boy philanderer, wore the cuckold's horns and didn't even know it. Elly dragged down anything in pants that came through the front door. She was more than fair game for deliverymen, door-to-door salesmen, canvassers, solicitors, and, all in all, whatever came close enough to trap.

That was a secret?

Roz butted her cigarette. Usually, she thought, she spent her time pitying Elly Carr. The poor pathetic creature—so much a victim of her own lusts that she couldn't control her urges, couldn't help giving in to whatever man presented himself.

The poor pathetic creature.

But who was pathetic now? Elly? Damn it, at least Elly had enough sex to keep her happy. Elly didn't sit around crying because she needed a man. Elly didn't burn up with frustration because her husband wasn't around to make the infernal itching go away. Elly scratched when she itched. When the urge set in—which it seemed to do at least three times a day, to judge from the past performance charts—Elly found a way to relieve it. If Ted wasn't handy, she selected another man. There was always some man handy, somewhere.

Maybe Roz was the poor, pathetic one.

No, she thought. No, this isn't the way it is. I'm Lincoln Barclay's wife. I belong to him and he belongs to me and that's all there is to it. He's my husband and I'm his wife. I don't play around because I need loving, not sexing. And what Elly Carr does isn't making love. She makes sex instead of love, and maybe that's fine for her, but it's not what I want. I'm not built that way.

I'm a woman, she told herself. I'm a woman, not a school girl, and I need to be loved. Just getting banged won't do it. I'm married to one man and he's the only man there is for me.

Period.

And when the slump was over, when Linc was a writer again and a man again, then everything would be all right again. Then the moon would beam and the sun would shine and the world would be golden. Then she would make love, not sex, and love would be a living force within her, and the world would whirl and the fulfillment would be sweet, very sweet.

Sweet.

She took out another cigarette, lighted it. She dragged deeply on the cylinder of paper and tobacco, took it from her mouth, stared at it. Her mind, slightly hysterical, saw new things in that one cigarette. If it were a little bit longer, the thought oddly, and a little bit thicker, and if it weren't burning . . ..

She laughed. She laughed happily and hysterically, and the laughter cut the edge of her frustration and made her whole again. It was amazing, the way laughter could do that for a person. You couldn't feel too sorry for yourself when you saw the humor of the situation. You couldn't wallow in self-pity when it was easier to throw your head back and roar with laughter. And, by the same token, you couldn't be very highly inflamed with desire when you were so busy laughing.

She smoked the cigarette, still chuckling softly to herself.

Elly Carr was at a party.

It was weekend in Cheshire Point, a venerable and venereal institution, and, as usual, Elly Carr was at a party. She was not especially certain whose party it was, and she was not at all certain what she was doing there, but there she was, by George, and in her hand was a martini glass, by gum, so she did the only thing possible under that set of circumstances.

She drained the martini. Most of it went into her mouth, and on down her throat, and eventually into her bloodstream, to remain there until it was screened out by her liver at the excruciatingly slow pace of an ounce per hour. Some of it, however, missed her mouth. The part which missed her mouth then dribbled down her chin and onto her dress. She tried to wipe it away, flailing her hand drunkenly, but she somehow only managed to slap frenetically at her breasts.

Which drew a little attention.

Almost at once there was a man at her elbow. She turned, staring at him but only half seeing him. He was a short man, with crew-cut black hair and thick horn-rimmed spectacles. As far as she knew, she had never seen him before in her life.

"You'll hurt yourself," he said.

"How?"

"Slapping yourself like that."

"Oh," she said. "Nope, doesn't hurt a bit. Could slap myself all day and it wouldn't hurt a bit."

"But—"

"See?" She slapped herself for emphasis, swatting her breast hard. This time it did hurt, strangely enough, and she clasped her hand to her breast, trying to soothe the pain. At the same time she looked into the eyes of the little man with the dark crew-cut and the horn-rimmed glasses, and this set up the usual chain reaction.

Sex.

She wanted him. It had happened that quickly—from drunken babbling to actual sexual desire. It was ridiculous, disgusting, but there was no way to deny the desire that existed now. It was genuine enough. She ached with want for him—want that had come quite literally out of the blue—and he was right there, and—

"I told you," the man said solicitously.

"Told me what?"

"That you'd hurt yourself. Hell, that's no way to wipe up a drink. You should get a sponge or something."

"Maybe."

"Or just let it evaporate."

"I suppose."

"Look," he said, "now you've gone and hurt yourself. Why don't we go somewhere so I can massage it for you?"

"But—"

"Just a gentle massage. Sure to do you a world of good. Nothing like an old breast massage to make you feel like a new woman."

A girl passed, carrying a tray with martinis on it. Elly traded her empty glass for a full one, drank off the gin, and replaced the glass on the tray all in one fluid motion. The short, dark, crew-cut, horn-rimmed man nodded at her with obvious approval. And equally obvious lust.

No, she thought. This was the wrong way to do it. It was okay with a salesman and okay with a delivery boy because the natives and the exurbanites didn't mingle. But when you started putting out for acquaintances at parties you were asking for trouble. Then word got back to your husband, and then the whole world started to fall in on you.

"Come on," he said. He was holding onto her arm.

"But—"

"You'll like it."

"I know damn well I'll like it."

"Then what's holding you back?"

"My husband."

The short man whirled around. "So you can go home with him. But first—"

The man touched her. That was nasty, Elly thought. The son of a bitch had to go and put one hand on her breast, damn him, and that was all she needed. It was enough before, without his hands on her. Now, with him touching her, it was horrible.

She needed him.

"Right through that doorway," he said persuasively, "there is a bedroom. It is empty now. We can go in there. We can lock the door, and no one will disturb us."

"How do you know?"

He looked at her, puzzled.

"About the bedroom," she went on. "You act as if you've been here before. Do you take many women into that bedroom?"

"Only my wife. Most of the time, that is. Sometimes other women, but generally my own wife."

"Huh?"

"I live here," the man said.

Elly nodded slowly. All the martinis were piling up now, and she was quietly bombed, and martinis were never noted as having a particularly repressing effect upon the libido.

"Your house," she said dully.

"That's right."

"You're the host."

"Uh-huh."

"It's your party."

"Sure, honey."

"Well," she said carefully, trying her best to avoid slurring her words, "that makes a difference. After all, it's only right to go to bed with the host. Like saying thank-you for the party, or something. Don't you think so, honey?"

"Sure," he said.

"Then let's go."

They went. He still held her arm, and now he led her across the floor, through the doorway, into a bedroom. He closed the door and turned around just as she was getting her bra off.

"Like?"

"Sure," he said.

"You're the host," she said. "I have to present my offerings for inspection, you see. For your approval."

"I think you're a little drunk, honey."

"I think I'm a lot drunk, honey."

"Come here."

She went to him. It was wrong, and she knew damn well it was wrong, but there was nothing she could do about it. He was her phantom lover for the time being just as sure as God made little green virgins, a phantom lover on a coal-black stallion, and she was stuck.

She had to go along for the ride.

Chapter 13

Linc Barclay sat in the tavern with the townies. The tavern was Early American in decor, with candle molders and foot warmers hanging incongruously from the ceiling, with plenty of old wooden paneling and wide board floors. The bartender drew a mug of ale and passed it to Linc. The townsfolk ignored Linc masterfully. It seemed at times that this was the townie's mission in life—to serve the commuter, to take the commuter's money, to make love on occasion to the commuter's wife, and then, ultimately, to ignore that same commuter when their paths happened to cross socially.

Linc did not concern himself with the philosophical aspects of the situation. He drank his ale. It was fine ale, and it went down smoothly. This was good. Everything else was pretty rough, and the smooth ale was a blessing.

He lighted a cigarette, took two drags, ground it out on the wide board floor under his heel. He asked for, and received, and paid for, another mug of ale. Which he drank.

He was a flop. Linc Barclay, Portrait of the Writer as a Young Flop. Man in a Slump. Man doing nothing with everything to do. Man—

Man who wasn't even a man. Man who couldn't make love to

his own wife because he was too hung up over everything else in the world. God, what was the matter with him?

He belonged at the typewriter, but he hadn't done a lick of typing in too long. He belonged with his wife, but here he was at the damned tavern drinking smooth ale and thinking unpleasant thoughts. He belonged elsewhere, and here he was, and to hell with it.

He had another mug of ale.

A jukebox, new and shining and not at all in keeping with the colonial air of the old tavern, gave forth with rock and roll. Linc scooped up his change, pocketed it, and headed for the door. He walked out into the night. His car was parked at the curb, but he sidestepped it and kept on walking. He was looking for something. He was not sure what he was looking for, but somewhere—

The girl fell in step with him at the corner of Vine and Dawson. She was a frail girl, looked about seventeen, with hollows under her eyes and very little flesh to her body. She looked hungry, as though she had not had a really fulfilling meal in days.

"Mister—"

He turned, studied her. She was trying to look sexy and it did not work at all. She was too young to look sexy, and too thin, and too hungry, and altogether too pathetic.

"You come with me, mister. I'll show you a good time."

He wanted to laugh at her. Sister, he thought, you're barking up the wrong fire hydrant. You couldn't show me a good time. I'm the no-action kid. See me when the slump ends.

"Any way you want it, mister. I go any way in the world. Just a couple dollars, sugar."

Mister had been better. The more intimate *sugar* was out of place on her thin bloodless lips.

"Mister—"

Not lust, he thought. Not lust, either because I am incapable of that emotion now or because she is incapable of arousing it. Not lust, certainly, but something else.

Pathos.

He reached into his pocket, found his wallet, drew out a five dollar bill. He gave it to the girl and her eyes brightened. She looked even younger now.

"Come on," she said. "I gotta room downtown. We'll have a ball, mister. We'll have ourselves a time."

"Keep the money," he said. "I can't come with you."

"What's the matter?"

"Nothing."

"I'm not good enough for you?"

He saw the pain in her eyes, the hurt, the injury. "No," he said carefully. "No, it's not that. But I've got a perfectly good wife at home. Go get yourself a meal."

He looked at her, saw the play of emotions across her face, saw injured pride give way slowly and be replaced by gratitude. Poor kid, he thought, she couldn't be a professional hustler, not wasting her time in Cheshire Point. Just a kid on the skids, a traveling kid with no money in her jeans and only one thing to offer, only one commodity to put on the market. He watched her scurry off toward the all-night diner, the five-dollar bill clenched tightly in her fist.

I've got a perfectly good wife at home. The sentence mocked him now. He had a perfectly good wife at home, but she was home and he was not, and she needed him while he remained unable to make her happy. What on earth was wrong with him?

Just a slump, he answered himself. And it was not a permanent thing. It would improve.

He found his way back to the tavern, got into his car. He started up the motor and drove slowly home. The slump would end. Soon, he hoped.

Soon.

Nan Haskell was at a party that Jenny and Les Cameron had had the temerity to throw. It was currently transforming the Cameron ranch house into something not far removed from a pigsty, and not even too far removed from the Augean stables. Nan sipped a Something Collins through a flavored straw and thought about Ted.

Who, for his part, was absent.

The Carrs were not at that particular party. The Carrs were never invited to the Camerons, and the Camerons in turn were never invited to the Carrs. Each had been frequently invited to the other home a year ago, but since then something had happened.

Nan, like everyone else in Cheshire Point, had a fair idea what had happened. It was never openly discussed, but general word had it that Ted Carr had said something to Jennifer Cameron, and that the something had been indiscreet, since Ted Carr had never been awarded medals for discretion. The various stories ran different courses from that point on. Some had it that Jenny had slapped Ted's face, and that was all. Others held that Jenny ran screaming to Les Cameron, who punched Ted in the nose. Still other versions had it that Les Cameron had walked into a bedchamber while Jenny and Ted were engaging in horizontal pleasantries.

The stories varied, but the point they made was simple enough. The Camerons and the Carrs were not friends any more because Ted had wanted to take Jenny to bed. Whether or not he had been successful was a moot point.

Now, Nan thought, he wants to take *me* to bed.

And he would probably succeed.

A woman was talking to her. She turned, spilling neither her Something Collins nor the ashes from her cigarette. She talked to the woman at her elbow, listened to a less-than-inspired monologue on the evils of crab grass and the impossibilities of keeping a crab-grass-free lawn. She replied, saying something innocuous, while trying to remember the woman's name. She failed, and by the time the name came back to her the woman was delivering the identical monologue to a man who looked about as interested as Nan had been.

Maybe the man, too, was thinking about adultery.

Because Nan was. She could think of nothing else. It was on her mind all the time now, along with Ted's voice over the telephone, and Ted's hands in the kitchen after the bridge game.

Howard could help her. Howard could pay more attention to her, and be more alive, and act more interested and interesting. Because, for the love of God, it was not as though she was in love with Ted Carr. Love? If she felt anything toward the man, it was a great deal closer to hatred than it was to love. She did not love him. She didn't care if he lived or died, would almost have preferred it if, in fact, he did die.

Then—

No, it was simple boredom. Ennui, *weltschmerz*, and the same thing in any language. Either way it smelled as sweet, and stank to high heaven. She was almost ready to spread her plump thighs for a man she did not even like, and just because she was bored.

She put out one cigarette and lighted another one. She took a deep breath, exchanged a few uninspired words about the weather with one man and parried half-hearted sex talk with another.

"How about it, Nan Haskell? Why don't you and I have a mad passionate affair?"

"I'd love to. But I'm afraid not, Mr. Thorpe."

"I don't appeal?"

"Of course you appeal. But you're one of those overworked executives. I wouldn't dare have a mad passionate affair with you."

"Why on earth not?"

"Because you might have a coronary attack and die in my arms."

"In your legs, you mean."

"Whatever. And we'd be the talk of Cheshire Point. Imagine what the minister would say!"

"You're absolutely right," he said, patting her thigh gently, almost paternally. "Besides, my insurance isn't paid up."

"Then we can't, Mr. Thorpe."

"Quite right, Mrs. Haskell. See me again, please do."

She moved off, picked up somebody's half-filled drink and finished it. There was a world of difference, she thought, between the sort of proposition Penn Thorpe had just handed her and the kind she'd gotten from Ted Carr. Ted was serious. Penn Thorpe, on the other hand, was making cocktail party passes, the perfunctory sort that flew through the air along with the gin fumes. They never stopped. They were the banter of Cheshire Point on weekends, the constant words that were always bandied about and never taken seriously. If she had accepted Penn's pass, he *would* have had a coronary, probably brought on by shock.

But Ted was different. He meant it.

Maybe I should get drunk, she thought. Maybe I could get stinking drunk, screaming drunk, barking drunk, and then I would go puke and Howard would take me home and that would solve everything.

She got stinking drunk.

She drank everything in sight, and she wound up throwing up over the rug, and Howard wound up taking her home. But even with her head spinning in circles, even with her stomach turning itself inside out, she knew full well that everything would not be solved, not at all.

The music on the phonograph was a Mozart piano sonata, simple and clean and precise, formal and crisp and cool. Roz Barclay sat on the sofa and smoked the last cigarette in the pack. Soon, she thought, she would have to get up and get another pack: She looked at the ashtray, overflowing with cigarette butts. Then she looked at the cigarette between the index and middle finger of her right hand. She remembered that last time she had studied a cigarette, remembered the thoughts she had thought then, remembered the laughter that had killed her frustrations for the time being.

Now she smoked, and listened to the music, and waited. The music was enough to carry her off, to occupy her mind so that most of her thoughts would cease to bother her. She was waiting for Linc. He would come home soon, and then they could be together. They could not make love, because lovemaking was out until Linc's slump ran its course. But they could be together. And simply being with the man you loved was a thousand times more satisfying than making love with a stranger.

She heard the car, ran to the window like a teenager waiting for a date. She saw the car pull into the driveway, then waited at the door for him to come back from the garage. He walked in, a strange faraway look in his eye. He kissed her and she hugged him.

"Okay?"

"Fine," he said.

"A little drunk?"

"Not even a little," he told her. "I had three mugs of ale downtown and walked around for a few minutes. This'll kill you."

"What will?"

"This," he said. "I ran into a whore."

"Anyone you knew?"

He laughed happily, then described the girl he had met. "A pathetic little thing," he said. "I gave her five dollars and sent her away. She couldn't have picked a less likely prospect."

She laughed with him. "Can we afford the five?"

"She needs it more than we do."

"I suppose so. Come on in. Sit with me."

He kissed her again. "What's playing?"

"Mozart."

"Nice. Let's warm the couch."

They sat together on the couch. For a long moment an urge spread on Roz, an urge to throw herself at this man, to do her damnedest to make him want her the way she wanted him. But the urge passed. She mastered it, and they sat quietly together and listened to the music.

A weekend in Cheshire Point. Sunday came, finally, and it was a day for black coffee and aspirin, a day to stay away from the children because noise was not a good idea when your head was a few sizes too large. It was a day for husbands and wives to forgive and forget, because Friday and Saturday night had undoubtedly supplied a great many scenes which needed forgetting as quickly as possible. It was a day to draw yourself together, a day to recuperate and set your sights on the week ahead, the week of commuting and school for the kids and everything else.

A weekend in Cheshire Point. It was hectic, and while you might look forward to it on Friday afternoon you regretted its arrival by Saturday morning and hated it all across the board by Sunday. It performed one function that could be described as valuable. It set you up for the work week.

Because, when Monday morning came around, you were glad.

CHAPTER 14

Monday morning came, and Maggie was glad of it.

She got up early enough to drive Dave to the station in the Volkswagen, then headed home again and stood under a cold shower until she felt sufficiently awake to eat breakfast. The weekend had been hellish, but it was over now, and today she and Elly were going into Manhattan to shop for clothes. She had not seen Elly since that Friday afternoon and she was anxious to see her, to talk to her, to be with her.

Friday itself had been more than she had expected. The bare-breasted episode was an unanticipated stroke of luck. She'd initiated it, of course, by stripping down to her bra, but when Elly had tugged her sweater over her head to reveal uncovered breasts, the ball had really gotten rolling. It wasn't hard to understand why Ell occasionally wandered around without a bra; the little devil had the firmest pair of breasts in captivity. Maggie's mouth had started watering at the sight of them, and concealing her interest had not been the easiest thing in the world.

But Friday afternoon had paved the way for the horrid weekend. She hadn't seen Elly, but she'd carried around the memory of Elly's exciting body, and as a result she'd been too keyed-up and stimulated to settle down. And so she had skipped Saturday night's round of parties. Instead she went into New York, went down to the Village to a convenient lesbian bar, and found a convenient pick-up.

The girl she picked up was a blonde bit of fluff, a student at Brooklyn College who was not, strictly speaking, a dyed-in-the-wool lesbian. The girl, Marcia Andover by name, was bisexual. She wore her hair in a long pony tail, wore a great deal of eye makeup, talked in self-consciously hip slang, and carried a copy of a book of poems by Alan Ginsberg under one arm. She was, in short, playing with hipsterism; she wanted to sample *kicks,* wanted to take her pleasure where she found it.

Maggie didn't like hit-and-run sex. But, at the moment, she had no choice; the afternoon with Elly had her ready to start climbing the walls, and a girl like Marcia could take a little of the tension out of her system. Marcia was ideal for her purposes. Marcia was attractive enough to be worth the trouble to get her into a bed, human enough to spend an evening with, and essentially dull enough so that Maggie would not miss her.

Maggie bought her drinks, talked to her about existentialist poetry, and went home with her to a third-floor walk-up on Barrow Street, a small single room in an old brownstone. There Marcia played progressive jazz records on a too loud hi-fidelity phonograph, danced around nude for awhile, and finally joined Maggie on top of the small bed.

They rubbed their breasts and bellies together, stroked each other, kissed and fondled each other. They were in bed together all night long, waking periodically to have sex, then drifting into a lazy sort of sleep only to awaken again and seek the delights of each other's bodies. It was a satisfying, fulfilling sort of evening, and when Maggie caught a northbound train in the morning, the tremendous wave of desire which Elly had caused had been temporarily slaked.

Still, as she finished her breakfast coffee this Monday morning, Maggie could not be too pleased with the way she had spent Saturday night. Marcia had been a substitute, and a mediocre one at best. Her breasts had been sweet to kiss, but they were not nearly so appealing as Elly's. Her body had been good to hold, but not nearly so good as Elly Carr's would be. Her moans and groans were exciting, certainly, but Maggie would be ten times as excited when it was Elly who was doing the moaning.

And now it was time to see Elly.

She called her first, on the phone. "It's Mag," she said. "Ready to go to the big town?"

"Very ready."

"I'll pick you up in ten minutes. Or is that too soon?"

"Better make it fifteen."

"Fine," Maggie said. "I'll drive the Volks and leave it at the station. See you in fifteen minutes, honey."

She put the receiver back on the hook. Then, whistling happily, she began to get dressed. She put on perfume. Just a little, just a dab behind each ear and at the tip of each breast. She did not want to overdo things, but she wanted to be as desirable as she possibly could.

Today would probably not be the day, but you could never tell. It might take quite awhile before she could even bring herself to toss a genuine pass at Elly. Then again, they might wind up in the rack within a day or two. There was no way to tell yet.

She smiled and hurried to the Volkswagen.

•   •   •

Something had happened over the weekend. Roz Barclay was not sure just what it was, or just how it had happened, but she could not deny that, whatever in hell it was, it had in fact occurred.

The weekend was a strangely quiet one for Roz and Linc Barclay. They did not go out to parties; when Linc was in a slump he was distinctly asocial, so they spent the weekend at home. Linc did not even drink. He sat around brooding, alternately reading any of a number of books, staring blankly at the screen of the television set, or lost in some private thoughts all his own.

Then Monday morning came. Linc was awake at nine—early for him. He headed for the bathroom, showered, shaved. He came out, dressed, in a tremendous hurry.

"Bring a thermos of coffee to the study when you get a chance," he said. "I'll be in there."

"You'll have breakfast first, honey. It won't take—"

"No, Roz. Not now. I think I'm going to be able to write. I don't want to pass up a chance. Just bring coffee."

She had known better than to argue with him. She went to the kitchen to make coffee while he went through the yard to the cottage he used for a study. She filled a thermos with the hot black liquid and took it to him, pausing at the door to listen to the hectic clatter of typewriter keys. It was a welcome sound, a sound she had gone too long without hearing. She listened for a moment, gauging the speed at which he was writing. He was going fast. That was a good sign, a sign that the slump was very probably over. He didn't have to grope for words. The sentences were flowing freely and easily, flowing from mind to paper with the typewriter an intermediary. She smiled to herself, a happy and grateful smile. Then, knowing better than to interrupt him by knocking, she pushed the door open.

She set the thermos of coffee upon the desk, unscrewed the top, used the top as a cup and filled it with coffee. He had not stopped typing. He came to the edge of a page, looked up only long enough to nod at her, then separated the sheet of carbon paper from the sheets he had just finished. He slapped the carbon paper between a fresh first and second sheet, rolled the paper sandwich into his typewriter, glanced for an instant at the last few words on the recently completed page, and started in again, picking up in the middle of the sentence and rattling away.

She watched him for several seconds. A cigarette was burning in the porcelain ashtray. Another cigarette was jammed in the corner of his mouth. He had not lighted this one yet, but he would get around to it sooner or later.

She left the cottage, walked back to the house. He was over it now, over the slump, through with sitting and moping and drinking too much. Now he would work at breakneck speed, finishing *Murder By Moonlight* easily within the week, working night and day, plunging into a fresh book or story as soon as the current one was finished. She didn't expect to see much of him for the next few days. He would be too busy catching up with himself, too busy pouring out all the words and phrases and sentences and paragraphs that had been bottled up for months, too busy grinding out all the pages he had not been able to write before.

But she did not mind. He was a writer and she was a writer's wife, and the clickety-clack of the IBM electric typewriter was the sweetest music she had ever heard.

CHAPTER 15

That morning, as she kissed Howard goodbye at the station, Nan Haskell watched Elly Carr kiss Ted goodbye and send him off to the wars of Madison Avenue. Then, driving home in the Chevy station wagon, she thought how thoroughly inconceivable it all was. Ted was Elly's husband and Howard was her husband, and it was absolutely out of the question that she would consider giving herself to Ted Carr.

It was all a dream, she decided. All a dream, or all a fantasy, or something of the sort. He had said—Friday, on the telephone—that he would see her Monday or Tuesday. But he had gone off on the 8:03 to New York and he would not be back until dinner time. He was not going to see her at all, was not going to make love to her, was not going to alter the overpowering boredom which was her life.

Maybe he just liked to talk. Maybe he got his kicks saying dirty words to women, grabbing hold of them and propositioning them. Maybe the years on Madison Avenue had made him far more concerned with advertising and promotion than with reality, far more with selling a girl on the idea of sex than with sex itself.

She was surprised, at twelve-thirty in the afternoon, to answer the door and find him on the steps.

"Hello, Nan-O."

"What are you—"

But he was pushing past her, stepping into the hallway, pulling the door closed behind him. She looked up, bewildered, and his smile leered back at her.

"You took the train—"

He reached out a hand and chucked her under the chin. "The trains," he said, "run both ways. Trains go to New York, and trains return from New York. Science is wonderful, Nan-O."

"But—"

"I took a train to New York. I took another train back from New York. Get your clothes off, dear heart. I want to go to bed with you."

"But—"

"Now."

It would not have happened like this with Howard. They would have embraced and she would have washed her face and brushed her teeth, and then he would have done the same. And she would have looked in on the children, making sure they were sleeping soundly, while he checked his attaché case to make sure all his paperwork was ready for the next morning. Then, clock set and lights out, they would go to bed.

But this was different. Fast directions, blind impulses. Nan was not excited now, not sexually aroused in the least, and yet she knew she had not the remotest chance of refusing to do whatever Ted Carr asked her to do. The boredom was over. Perhaps boredom was preferable to what was going to come next, perhaps monotony was a better alternative than misery. It made little difference. He would command and she would follow orders, and, to mix a metaphor hopelessly, the chips could fall as they might. Or may. Or something like that—

"Take off your clothes," he said.

"Not here, Ted. Somebody might see. We could go to the bedroom. We could—"

"No one can see in, Nan-O. Get nude, and fast."

She knew better than to argue. She stood there, feeling half like a fool and half like a goddess of love. She was wearing an ugly housedress that had a row of silly buttons from the neckline to the hem. There must have been two dozen of the buttons, and she opened them one at a time, her fingers quick but deliberate. She stepped out of the dress, finally, smiling a smile of self-satisfaction, standing before him in bra and panties and house slippers. Her eyes were shining. She tossed her shoulders back, thrusting her big breasts at him, and suddenly, all at once, the passion began to reach her, to flood her system.

It was uncanny. She had begun stripping, feeling not at all sexy, feeling not remotely passionate. But the simple act of removing the dress, of submitting to this sandy-haired man's strong will, had an aphrodisiacal effect upon her. Her whole body was tingling with sexual excitement now. She was in her own living room, standing near-nude before another woman's husband, about to commit the first act of infidelity of her life. And she was not scared, was not guilt-ridden, was not disturbed.

She was excited.

"More," he said, his voice slightly hoarse. "God, you've got big ones, Nan-O. Take the bra off."

She took the bra off. Her breasts sprang out, free and unbound, and his eyes feasted upon them. He walked toward her, eyes bright, and reached out a hand. He flicked the nipple of one proud breast with his forefinger and she drew in her breath sharply.

"Nice, Nan-O. Let's see what else you got. Get your pants off. I want to see all of you."

She stepped out of her panties. He came still closer and caressed her momentarily again. She quivered with intense excitement. Howard hadn't made her feel like this in years. She'd had sex and had enjoyed it, had achieved climax time and time again. But now the half-caresses Ted was giving her were working her to peaks of pleasure she'd never known.

"You'd better take your shoes off," he said. "You look funny as hell."

She kicked off the house slippers. He was still fully dressed, wearing a foulard tie and a brown herringbone tweed suit, and the incongruity of standing stark naked in front of this fully dressed man should have been something to laugh at. With the proper caption, the tableau of which she was a part could have appeared as a cartoon in *Playboy,* maybe in the *New Yorker.* And yet she found nothing to laugh at.

He took off his clothes, hanging tie and jacket over a doorknob, folding his trousers very neatly and placing them on a chair, putting his cashmere-and-nylon socks in his brown pebble-grain loafers. Now he, too, was naked. He placed his hands on his hips and leered at her. His eyes traveled from her face to her feet, making a slow journey with several side trips along the way. His glance set her on fire. She could feel his eyes on her skin and they made her tingle.

"Let your hair down, Nan-O."

It was in a bun. "Don't you like it this way?"

"One bun is enough. Let it down, Nan-O."

She let her hair down. It came cascading over her bare shoulders, soft and golden, framing her flushed face. He moved closer to her now and she could feel body heat. He reached out, touched her face.

"You want it," he said. "Don't you?"

"Yes."

"You want it badly."

"Yes!"

"Tell me about it. Tell me how much you want it, Nan-O. Tell me what you want me to do to you."

She told him.

He reached for her breasts and gripped firmly. "Not like that," he said. "Get down on your knees. And tell me dirty, Nan-O. Use nasty words."

She sank to her knees and looked up at him. She told him the things he wanted to hear and used the words he wanted her to use. She watched the visible evidence of his passion mount with lust. Then his hands were on her shoulders, shoving her backwards. She fell down on the floor and he was advancing on her, his eyes wild.

"Not here," she whispered. "Upstairs, in bed. Not here—"

He took her there, on the living room floor. He surged into her like waves piling up on a rocky coast, plummeted into her, stabbed wildly at her. He hurt her but she did not mind the pain, and he made her feel like a woman being taken, made her feel fully alive for the first time in far too long.

The peak, when she reached it, was strange and wonderful. At apex she shrieked loud and long, squealing like a virgin impaled upon a fiery sword.

And then it was over.

He left her without a word. He stood up and got dressed while she lay upon the floor, eyes closed, breathing shallow. He walked out and she remained there, alone in space and time. She was an adulteress now. She had sinned. She had betrayed her husband.

She felt wonderful.

"I've got some eggs for you," Roz Barclay said. "Scrambled, the way you like them. And crisp bacon, and more coffee. And toast with jam. You must be starving."

Linc looked up from the typewriter, smiled. "You're an angel," he said. "And your halo makes a lovely symbol."

"Save the line," she suggested.

"I used it in the last chapter. Pass the food, angel."

He attacked the eggs and bacon almost viciously, shoveling food into his mouth and down his throat. "I'm really cooking now," he said between bites. "Thirty-five pages already. The book is rolling along and gathering no moss."

"And you're enjoying it?"

"I always enjoy it when it goes like this. Hell, I've got to make up for lost time."

"I know."

"And I just got a hell of a notion," he went on, pausing to sip coffee from the cap of the thermos jug. "Make a good slick yarn, probably go to the *Post* or *McCall's*. As soon as I get this damn book out of the way I'll run it through the typewriter and see what comes out. I'm glad you brought me a plate of food, honey. I've got a feeling this is going to be a long siege. I may be going all night."

She arched an eyebrow.

"Well," he said, "maybe not *all* night."

She grinned.

"Because," he said, "when I'm in a slump, I'm in all the way. And when I come out of a slump—"

Her grin widened. "I'll get back to the house now, Linc. I'm keeping you from your work. When should I . . . expect you?"

"Any time."

"No idea when?"

"No idea," he said. "But don't wear anything under your dress. That way we'll save a little time."

Elly and Maggie ate lunch at the top of the Tishman Building, the glass and steel skyscraper at 666 Fifth Avenue.

They had dinner in a cellar restaurant on Bleecker Street.

The decision to stay for dinner had been a pleasant one, suggested by Maggie and agreed to readily enough by Elly. They had had lunch, had shopped for awhile on Fifth Avenue without buying anything, then headed west to Broadway. *A Sound Of Distant Drums,* the hit drama based on the Westlake kidnaping, was playing at the Cort; for the hell of it, Maggie went to the box office to see if any tickets were available for that evening. There was a pair on hand, front and center in the orchestra.

"Let's take them," Maggie said.

"But—"

"Dave won't mind if I stay in town. Neither will Ted—just give him a ring and ask him to take Pam out for dinner. It'll be a treat for the kid and a treat for us."

Ted wasn't there, which made it that much simpler. She left a message with his secretary, then waited while Maggie put a call through to Dave Whitcomb. Then more shopping, and a stop for drinks, and a cab down to the simply wonderful little Italian restaurant that Maggie liked, and plates of lasagna with icy chianti. Elly couldn't remember feeling so completely at ease. Yes, she thought, Maggie's friendship was going to prove valuable. If anything would ever control her sexual excesses, Maggie would. Now, with Maggie, she felt no need for a phantom lover, no need for a deliveryman or a door-to-door salesman. She was at ease, relaxed, completely at peace with the world and with herself.

They caught a cab and rode to the Cort. "This is funny," Elly said. "It feels like . . . like a date. Do you know what I mean?"

"Uh-huh."

"Of course we're hardly dressed for the occasion."

"You look fine, Ell."

"Thanks. But I look fine for a shopping splurge at Saks, not for an evening on the town. Everybody will stare at us."

"They won't," Maggie said. "They may think we're tourists from Peoria, but they won't stare at us. Besides, who cares if they do?"

"Not I," Elly said gaily. "They can stare until their eyes bulge. Whee! We're on a date, Mag."

"Uh-huh. Maybe we should neck in the back seat of the cab."

"Wonderful," Elly said. "After the show we'll have our cabby drive through Central Park. And we'll neck like high school kids. Okay?"

"Fine with me."

A Sound Of Distant Drums turned out to be all the critics had said it was. Elly let herself get lost in the play, let herself become absorbed by characters and dialogue. When the final curtain fell she had to shake herself in order to remind herself that she was in a theatre, that the action which had transpired was action on a stage and not the real thing.

Then they were outside, in the middle of after-the-theatre pedestrian traffic on Broadway. They ducked into a bar for drinks and had two each, enough to get Elly a little bit high again.

"This is fun," she said earnestly. "So much fun."

"I know it is."

"You want to know something? I don't even want to go home. I want to stay here in Manhattan until hell freezes. Maybe even longer."

"That's a long time."

"I know it. Maggie, I don't even want to call Ted. I just want to stay."

"We could stay the night, you know. We could go to a hotel."

"Let's! Oh, it's an adventure, Mag. I need an adventure."

"Well have one," Maggie promised, her eyes gleaming strangely. "But first call Ted so he doesn't worry. Then we'll have our adventure. We'll go to a night club or two and get stinking drunk and stay over at a hotel. Sound like fun?"

"Sounds heavenly," Elly said. "Whee! An adventure!"

Chapter 16

Roz Barclay sat reading in a comfortable chair. The book in her hand had been written by a fellow with whom Linc had been friendly years ago. When they all lived in Manhattan, the writer and his wife and Linc and Roz were a frequent foursome. Now, while Linc and Roz had moved to northern Westchester, the other writer and his wife had wound up in Bucks County, in Pennsylvania. Both families lived within commuting distance of New York, but in opposite directions. They never saw each other any more.

The book was a rather moody novel about a disturbed teenager, and only loyalty to a writer who had been a close friend kept Roz from putting the book down unfinished. She plowed onward, hoping at least to be able to save Linc the monumental chore of reading the thing. This way she would finish it herself and tuck it away in the bookcase, and if he ever asked about it, she would tell him how rotten it was.

Because, for the time being, Linc did not have time to waste reading lousy books. He had his own lousy books to write.

And he would be coming to her soon. She shuddered in delighted anticipation, knowing that soon he would come to her, taking a break from the book to bring another slump to its end. He had told her not to wear anything under her dress, saying it would save time. And she was not wearing anything under her dress. When he came she could throw the dress over her head and be naked for him, nude for him, ready for him. Then he could take her, quickly and passionately and breathlessly, and the world could pour itself into a deep pit and dash itself to fragments.

Her eyes were busy with the bad book about a disturbed adolescent. But her mind and her body waited for Linc.

Elly was having a wonderful time.

She and Maggie were at a front table in Endsville, a progressive jazz club on the East Side. On the stand, an instrumental quartet was working wild changes on "I've Got Rhythm." The original melody had disappeared, and the four Negroes were swinging with the basic chord structure, twisting the song through new and wonderful channels.

Elly listened to the drums, to the bass. The drummer worked the top cymbal, keeping the beat steady, playing on top of the beat. The bassist moved up and down the chord patterns, backing the group. She looked at the pianist, then at the tenor sax. The music was wild and her ears and brain were filled with it.

"Maggie," she said, "this is fun."

"You're enjoying yourself?"

"I'm having a ball."

"You like the music?"

"I love the music. I haven't had this much fun in . . . in years. I'm glad we decided to stay in the city. This beats the damn train home and quitting early."

Maggie smiled, and Elly noticed again just how beautiful the red-haired girl was. So beautiful, and so good to her, and so good for her, and so much fun to be with.

"When you're having a good time," Maggie said, "there's no point in stopping early."

"I know."

"We'll stay here for another drink or two. Then we'll find someplace else to go. I already made reservations at the Hasbrouck House. Our room is waiting for us any time we want to go there. So we don't have to worry about finding a place to stay. We can paint the town scarlet all night long."

"Sounds like fun."

"It is fun, Ell."

She got lost in the music again. The tenor man unwound with a long solo, gutty and bluesy, and she let her mind float along on the ribbon of pure melody, let herself get immersed in the music. When the solo ended she saw Maggie ordering another round of drinks.

"Not for me, Mag."

"Of course for you. I can't drink them both all by myself, Ell. One's for me and one's for you."

"I'm pretty well stoned already, Maggie. I don't want to pass out. I'd make a fool of myself."

"No fool like a pretty fool, Ell."

"I'm tipsy, Mag—"

Maggie's hand moved across the table, caught Elly's wrist, held it. "Don't you worry," she said. "We're out on the town, sweetie. We've got a perfectly good right to get stoned."

"I suppose so."

"So you just drink your drink, Ell. We'll stay here until the band takes a break. Then maybe we'll take a hansom ride through Central Park. You know, one of the old horse cabs."

"I've never been in one of those, Mag."

"They're fun."

She looked at Maggie. Her eyes were bright now, alive. She sipped her drink and studied the red-haired girl over the brim of her glass. She was all keyed up, all excited.

"And we can neck in the back," she said, giggling a little. "Like on a date. Can't we, Maggie?"

"Of course, sweetie."

Something was a little funny, she thought. Something was a little bit out of the ordinary.

She pushed the thought from her mind and finished her drink.

It was a Monday night, of course. And, since it was a Monday night, Howard Haskell had brought work home from the office. He'd taken a later train than usual from New York, and he'd hardly said a word through dinner, and now he was locked up in his den with the tentative plans for some advertising campaign or other.

And Nan was alone.

The boys were sleeping. Nan ate in front of the television set, which was not even turned on, and felt lonely. Lonely and wretched and unhappy. And, at the same time, alive.

Ted Carr.

Ted Carr, and the sordid and cheap affair in which he was her partner, was making a monumental difference in her life. Already, after one horrible and yet somehow wonderful love-bout in the middle of her own living room floor in the middle of the afternoon, the monotony had fled from her existence like bugs from a room sprayed with DDT. She was not just a wife, not just a mother.

She was a mistress.

A mistress. The word had a strange and unfamiliar ring to it. It didn't seem possible that such a word could be properly applied to solid citizen Nan Haskell, mother of two, pillar of Cheshire Point. And yet it was true. She had given herself to Ted, had begged him on her knees to take her, had asked for him in vulgar words, had made a slave out of herself, a slave to his whims and passions.

And it was not a one-shot arrangement. She knew this, knew it for a fact, knew it as well as she knew her own name. It was autumn in Cheshire Point and she was somewhere in the middle of an illicit affair. In the fall a young wife's fancies lightly turn to thoughts of sex, she thought. In the fall a young wife starts putting out for a neighbor.

In the fall—

It might have been different if Howard had not had a satchel full of work that night. Maybe that was just an excuse, maybe the affair with Ted was destined to run its course no matter what, but she somehow could not help feeling that if Howard had been able to spend time with her that very evening, if he had been more talkative and more ... loving, she might have been able to get back on the right track.

It was a moot point now. She who had been so one-hundred per cent faithful was now unfaithful, and the act of infidelity would be repeated as long as it was valuable to her. She had been bored; she was bored no longer. She had been in a rut; the rut had now turned into a groove. She had been tired, miserable, plodding along without any interruption of what had developed into a less-than-bearable routine.

Now all that was changed.

Ted Carr, sandy-haired, smiling, determined. Not so handsome as Howard, not at all as nice as Howard, not as desirable a mate as Howard, but somehow far more important than Howard could ever be, far more essential to her well-being.

And she would let the affair run its course. In time it would burn itself out, and she would be Howard Haskell's faithful wife once more, and everything would be hunky-dory again. But for the time being she would be everything Ted Carr wanted her to be, would do everything he wanted her to do, would lower herself into muck and make herself worse than a whore if he ordered her to do so. He was her excitement, her dynamism, almost her whole life.

This is wrong, she thought. This is all very wrong, and I should be heartily ashamed of myself. I should hate myself.

I do hate myself.

But that was immaterial. She had a need for Ted which she could not deny. She was in a flimsy canoe in rocky waters, but she was also on one hell of a wild boat ride.

CHAPTER 17

They found the old-fashioned cab at 59th Street and Fifth Avenue, at the eastern foot of Central Park. The driver, all decked out in livery, spoke softly and charmingly in a mild British accent. His horse was something of a glue factory candidate, but in the moon and star light he was magically transformed into something dashing, into a sleek black stallion with hooves of steel and fiery eyes.

The same black stallion, Elly thought fleetingly, on which her phantom lover always rode.

She put the thought out of her mind. The night was young and she felt very beautiful, and now she was sitting beside Maggie Whitcomb in the old hansom while the horse was clip-clopping through pathways in Central Park, while the old liveried driver dozed with the reins in his hands. She smelled the good healthy horse smell, inhaled with it the country fragrance of Central Park. She heard muted traffic sounds in the distance, the sounds of New York by night, sounds which suggested home to her much more strongly and much more convincingly than the cricket chirping you heard in bed at Cheshire Point.

"Happy, Ell?"

"Completely happy."

"I like Central Park, Ell. An oasis in the middle of the Manhattan desert. It's peaceful."

"Uh-huh." She leaned back, closing her eyes. Maggie was wearing perfume and the smell was strong now, strong but subtle. She let her head loll back on Maggie's shoulder. "I lived near the park," she said. "When I was a kid we lived in the West Seventies just a block from the park. I used to play here all the time."

"It must have been fun."

"It was."

Silence, broken by traffic in the distance, horse hooves in front. Maggie's arm went around her shoulder, holding her.

"We're on a heavy date," Maggie whispered. "Now we have to neck."

"I almost forgot."

"Kiss me, Ell."

"I've never kissed a girl before."

"Then let me be the first."

Maggie's lips were wonderfully soft. The kiss started as a peck but grew into something a little more. Elly felt Maggie's arms around her, holding her close. She tasted the incomparable sweetness of Maggie's warm mouth.

"That was . . . nice, Maggie."

"You must have been a wonderful date. I bet all the boys liked to neck with you, Ell."

"They did more than that. I was a very easy lay."

"You were?"

Something made her go on. "I would put out for any boy who asked me. I was a tramp, I guess."

"Boys take advantage of a girl, Ell."

"I know. Oh, I'm tipsy, Maggie. I'm drunk."

"You won't be sick, will you?"

"No, but I'm drunk. Why don't you kiss me again, Maggie? I want to be kissed now. I feel all funny inside. Please kiss me."

Maggie's mouth came to hers. Maggie's arms were firmer around her now, and she felt Maggie's breasts press in close against her own breasts. She opened her mouth automatically and Maggie's warm tongue stole inside, caressing her lips, making her whole mouth tingle. She suddenly remembered the way Maggie's bare breasts had looked Friday afternoon, remembered the way the two of them had sat around drinking Scotch with their bosoms showing.

The memory sent a jolt of inexplicable passion racing through her. She was warm all over, her cheeks warm from all the drinks and her loins warm with rising lust. She tightened her own grip around Maggie, ran her fingers through Maggie's long red hair. The hair was the texture of spun silk, good to touch, good to run your fingers through. Her own tongue darted forward to meet Maggie's tongue and the contact was purely electric in its intensity. She was charged up now, stimulated.

"Maggie—"

"Hold me, Ell. Hold me close."

"This is silly, isn't it? We're both girls and we're necking and kissing and hugging. I like this, though, even if we are silly. I like the way you feel, Maggie. You have the most wonderful breasts."

"Do you like them?"

"I'm going to touch them to show you how much I love them, Maggie. Oh, God, they feel so nice! Is it wrong to touch another woman's breasts? I never did anything like this before."

"It's not wrong."

"Because they feel so *nice!* I wish I had breasts like yours, Maggie. Big and firm."

"Yours are lovely, Ell."

"Do you think so?"

She felt Maggie's hands moving, finding her own breasts and holding them tenderly. The touch excited Elly. She began to tremble. She did not know what was happening to her but it was something phenomenal, something wonderful. Her body was on fire.

"When I saw you Friday," Maggie was saying, "Your breasts. I wanted you to touch me and I wanted to touch you."

"Why, Maggie?"

"I don't know why. Hold me close, Elly. Kiss me."

A kiss that made her head swim. Maggie's hands, active, clever, one hand toying tenderly with her breasts, the other stroking her legs.

"Maggie—"

"What, Ell? What, my darling?"

"Is it wrong, Maggie?"

A pause.

Then: "Do you like this, Ell?"

"Oh, yes."

"And this? Do you like what I'm doing to you now, my darling? Do you like the way it makes you feel?"

"Yes!"

"And this?"

"Oh, yes! Yes, God, yes, yes, yes!"

"Then it can't be wrong, Ell. It can't be wrong."

•   •   •

The door opened. Linc Barclay came through the door, his shirt unbuttoned, his eyes bloodshot and rimmed with dark circles. He came through the door in a hurry, and he reached Roz just as she rose to meet him, and his arms encircled her and drew her so close to him that she gasped. He kissed her, his mouth sure and demanding, and she returned his kiss with all the passion she felt for him.

His hands roamed her body. She quivered with delight, and she went limp with lust, and his hands were clever.

He said: "Good girl. Nothing under your dress, is there?"

"Just me, Linc."

"That's all I'm interested in. Bed, Roz."

No words. They raced up the stairs, and they tore off their clothes, and they were together. And the slump was over, the slump was most assuredly over, the slump was magnificently banished. He took her, needing her, wanting her, possessing her, and the world was aflame with beauty.

This made everything, all of it, worthwhile. It was the whole world, and Roz felt herself submerged in boiling waters, tossed here and there, exploding in passion that was unlike anything that had ever happened. She was with her man, the only man she had ever loved, the only man she could ever possibly love. She was with her man, and this was the way it ought to be, this was the way it had to be, this was in fact the only way it could ever be.

This justified everything. This made the world worthwhile, and it made the hard times worthwhile, and it made the dry periods and the slump bearable. This was everything, the total experience of humanity, and it was nothing short of perfect.

It lasted almost forever.

Then the end came. The end, with the world going up in bloody smoke, with bodies rising and falling, tempos increasing, everything emphatically right for once and for all. The end, and an end so perfect it was also a beginning, an end which was a promise.

They stayed in bed for a few minutes. They shared a single cigarette in the darkness, and they said no words because no words were necessary. They had no need for words; words were a commodity of Linc's, a marketplace item which he sold at so much a throw. Words were unnecessary between lovers, between man and wife. They were unimportant.

And then he got up, finally, and dressed. He was going back to work; she knew this without having to ask. She waited while he left the house and returned to the studio. Then she went downstairs to get a fresh pot of coffee ready. He would be working all night, and he would need plenty of black coffee to keep him going.

When she paused at the door of the study she heard the typewriter going a mile a minute.

The Hasbrouck House was not far from Central Park, not far from where their driver let them out. Maggie paid him ten dollars, led Elly along the few blocks to the hotel. It was a primarily residential hotel, its prices moderate, its service quietly elegant, its rooms pleasant. Maggie had been there before, with a lesbian lover. The hotel, while not by any means specifically catering to the gay trade, cast a tolerant eye on homosexual love affairs. As such it was an obvious choice of a place to spend the evening.

Because, Maggie knew, the seduction of Elly Carr was no long-range proposition, not now. It was something to be accomplished as quickly as possible, something to be attended to that very night. Elly was drunk enough so that her inhibitions did not stand in her way, and she was hot enough so that she would love what Maggie was going to do to her. And she was beautiful and desirable and sweet, so much so that Maggie had to have her or drop dead of desire.

A bellhop showed them to their room. Maggie locked the door, and she turned to Elly, and the little brunette came into her arms at once, nuzzling her sweet face against Maggie's big breasts.

"Let's get out of our clothes, my darling."

"Yes, Maggie. Oh, yes."

"I want to see your bare breasts again. I want to touch them this time, Ell. I want to kiss them."

"Oh, God."

She unzipped Elly's dress and helped her out of it. She unclasped Elly's bra, then took off her own clothing. She watched Elly peel down her underpants and caught her breath at the sight of Elly's beautiful naked body. The girl, stark naked, was even more lovely than Maggie had dared to imagine.

"Kiss me, Maggie."

Maggie did not need an invitation. She took the girl close, held Elly in her arms and when their bare breasts came together both girls moaned as if they had touched a live wire. Maggie's nipples were firm little jewels now that drilled fiery holes in Elly's breasts. They stood up, and they drank each other in deep kisses, and then they were on the bed and in each other's arms.

"Lie still," Maggie whispered. "I'm going to make you feel like an angel, Elly. Ell, Ell, Ell—I'm going to make you see the other side of the moon. Hold onto your hat, darling!"

Her mouth touched Elly's mouth. Her tongue sank in, kissing with passion. Then her lips brushed Elly's closed eyes, nuzzled her throat. Elly was in the grip of passion. Maggie could take her time, could do everything as she wanted it to be done. There was no question of seduction. The seduction such as it was had been accomplished.

She kissed Elly's breasts.

Maggie was a woman, and she knew what a woman's body was, knew how to excite it, knew how to make it respond. She kissed Elly's breasts with her lips and tongue, let her hot tongue glide over skin that was silk-soft, sucked the sweet nipples until they throbbed with passion.

Elly was moaning now.

She stroked and kissed Elly's legs. Elly had lovely legs, lovely thighs, and she kissed them.

And then the finale. Then the moon and the stars, and life and death, and the overall end of the world.

They slept, body against body, breasts close to breasts. They slept in love.

CHAPTER 18

Tuesday morning was traumatic. Now you might argue that morning is by definition a traumatic state for most people, and you might well be correct arguing thus. But for Elly Carr, who opened her eyes in her room at the Hasbrouck House a few minutes after seven, Tuesday morning was infinitely more traumatic than usual.

There was the hangover. That was fine for a starter. It was a hangover with bells on. Literally. Elly could hear the bells booming inside her skull, and with no effort at all she could imagine the hunchback Quasimodo doubled up somewhere in her cranial cavity, pulling a rope and giggling in hunched hysterics.

A hangover is no picnic. A hangover like Elly's, which is as much like an ordinary morning-after headache as a nuclear explosion is like a firecracker, is even less of a festive occasion. But in this particular instance, the hangover was nothing at all. Elly barely noticed it.

Maggie eclipsed the hangover. Maggie was lying flat on her back, eyes closed, breasts pointing ceilingward, red hair sprawled out over a white pillowcase. There was Maggie, and there was Elly, and the room reeked with the pungent odors of stale sex.

Sex.

Sex with Maggie, yet.

Homosexual sex.

Sexual homosexual sex.

Lesbianism, for the love of God!

Some people, when they drink to excess, experience what is popularly known as a blackout. In the morning, when their eyes unwillingly open, they remember very little of what transpired the night before. In place of memories, these persons have huge spaces of blankness.

This can be unpleasant. A man may drink, behave like a total ass, and wake up not realizing he has made a mortal enemy of a former friend. But there are good things about a blackout. Sometimes memories are not worth having.

Elly Carr never blacked out. This morning was, in that respect if in few others, no different from many other mornings. Elly remembered everything she had done the night before, remembered every last detail from the moment Maggie picked her up at her house in Cheshire Point, driving to the railroad station in the little Volkswagen, to the last final and penultimate quiver of orgasmic fury in the bed at the Hasbrouck House.

These memories were less than a delight.

Elly shuddered violently. She tried to imagine what on earth had made her do what she had done, tried to figure out some vaguely rational explanation for the undeniable fact that she and Maggie had made love. There was no such explanation. It was impossible, ridiculous, absurd. It made no sense at all. But it had happened.

She sat up shakily. Maggie was still asleep, and Elly was glad of it; the morning was bad enough alone and could only be worse if shared with another human being. Especially, she thought, Maggie Whitcomb.

There was a pack of cigarettes on the nightstand. She reached for the pack, shook a cigarette loose, placed it between her lips. Lips which had kissed Maggie last night. Lips which had—

She found matches and scratched one. Her hands were shaking rather violently by now and she had a little trouble getting the flame and the cigarette end together. She managed it, eventually, shook out the match with a flick of her wrist and let it fall to the carpet. She sucked smoke into her lungs, letting it trail out from between slightly parted lips.

It had happened. And, what was more, she had enjoyed it. That was the most singly frightening fact of all. The act itself was tough enough to accept, but a person is never entirely responsible for what happens when he or she is drunk, and if she and Maggie had simply fooled around foolishly for a few minutes, it would be easy enough to rationalize the whole thing as something which was meaningless and not worth thinking about.

But she had loved every minute of it.

And so had Maggie.

What in hell did it mean? That she was a . . . lesbian? God, it didn't seem possible! She was a nympho, maybe; she was the easiest lay in the western hemisphere, perhaps. But a lesbian? It was only common sense to assume that a girl who yanked her skirt up every time a man was in the neighborhood was hardly the type to get hot for girls.

But—

Hold on, she thought. Leave us be logical, little girl. Painfully logical, if the need be. Because, no matter how many ways you find to avoid the issue, the fact remains that you went to bed with Maggie. And that you had a feeling, somewhere deep down inside you, that it was going to happen. And that you were pretty damned glad when it *did* happen, and that you loved it, and that now you wish it hadn't happened but you still loved every minute of it while it was going on.

And that you want it to happen again.

She drew on the cigarette. Did she want it to happen again? Now *there* was a question. Questions were easy to find—they were cropping up all over the place. But answers were something else entirely. It wasn't so very easy to pick out the answers to all those interesting questions.

Questions and answers. Problems and headaches, and the hangover in back of all of it, making everything worse. And a tremendous thirst, with her throat parched. There was a private bathroom attached to the room, and there was running water in the sink, but she didn't have the strength to get up and slake her thirst.

She was on her third cigarette when Maggie awoke.

Maggie actually was awake before she opened her eyes. Consciousness returned slowly, and while it was returning she remained motionless, nude upon her back. She stayed there for several minutes, taking stock of where she was and how she had gotten there, listening to the quiet sounds of Elly smoking a cigarette.

Then, finally, she opened her eyes, stretched, and sat up.

Elly blushed.

Maggie looked at the girl. A whole rush of emotions came to her . . . pity for Elly, who was obviously tormented and miserable, guilt at having made a lesbian out of her, whether for a night or longer, and, beneath it all, the undercurrent of desire that refused to be dispelled.

She said: "Good morning."

"Maggie . . ."

"Don't say anything," she said. "Not for a few minutes, anyway. Let me talk. I've got something to tell you."

"Maggie . . ."

"I mean it, Ell. Let me get it all out. It's not easy to say. Then you can talk all you want."

"Whatever you say."

She swallowed. It was not easy, not at all. Because now honesty was going to have to be the best policy. She had been as cold-blooded as possible in the now-successful campaign to get in bed with Elly Carr; now, the battle won, she had to be honest. She was not fundamentally a cold-blooded person. Sexual conquest alone was not enough for her. She was emotional, and if this whole affair with Elly was going to amount to anything more than simple one-shot sex, she was going to have to play the game according to the rules, with no low blows and no concealed weapons.

So she said: "I'm a lesbian, Ell. I've been exclusively homosexual since I was a junior in prep school. I've never slept with a man, because my husband, David, is a male homosexual. We—"

"Maggie—"

"Hear me out. Dammit, I said not to interrupt. Will you let me finish what I'm trying to say!"

"I'm sorry."

"I didn't mean to snap at you. Ell, Dave is gay and I am gay and we're married to keep up appearances. And I . . . I seduced you, honey. I very willfully got you to accept me as a friend, and then I just as willfully got you to . . . to go to bed with me. Maybe it was wrong of me. I'm not certain, and maybe that's something you can decide better than I can.

"I'll tell you this much, Ell. I wouldn't have tried to make love to you unless I thought you would be responsive. I got you drunk last night, but I still wouldn't have done anything if I hadn't known damned well that you wanted it as much as I did. And while we were making love it meant as much to you as it did to me. I know that."

Elly didn't say anything, and Maggie paused, searching the brunette's face, trying to find some indication that her words were having an effect. Elly's face was blank. It told her nothing. She reached for one of Elly's cigarettes and lighted it, using the time the act of lighting the cigarette took to reorganize her thoughts.

"I knew you had . . . homosexual leanings," she said finally. "All along, you were a potential lesbian. Otherwise nothing could have happened between us, Ell."

"What do you mean?"

"Think back," she said. "Remember the afternoon when we sat around—uh—a little exposed? Didn't you feel anything?"

"Maybe I did."

"And you suggested necking in the cab. It was just a joke, but you thought of it all by yourself. Deep down inside you weren't joking, Ell. Subconsciously you knew what you were and knew what I was. And you knew what you wanted."

"It's hard to believe, Maggie."

"It's true, though."

"Then I'm a . . . a lesbian? I've been one all along?"

"Yes."

And Elly was leaning forward, unconscious of her own nakedness, intent solely upon making a point. "Then you listen for a moment," she said. "Because I've got a thing or two to tell you."

Maggie listened. She listened to an absolutely incredible story of nymphomania, of sordid trysting, of blatant adultery. She listened to the recounting of a saga starring deliverymen and handymen and door-to-door salesmen, a story of a phantom lover on a black stallion, a story of deep impulses and frighteningly intense emotions.

"My God," she said. "I wouldn't have believed it, Ell."

"Nobody knows. I've never told anybody. I almost went to a psychoanalyst once but I knew I would have to tell him what my problem was and I couldn't bring myself to say a word to anyone, not even a doctor. Now do you think I'm a lesbian, Maggie? Maybe I'm just oversexed. Maybe I'm some kind of sex maniac or something."

"You're a lesbian, Ell."

"But—"

"Don't you see?" She leaned forward, ready to make her point. It was so obvious and Elly couldn't understand it. "You've never really been satisfied by men, Ell. Not inside, not all the way. That's why there's this phantom lover image in the background. That's why you keep searching for the perfect lover, letting these rotten men walk all over you. And that's why it never worked, why you couldn't straighten out. Deep down inside you wanted a woman. You wanted me, Ell."

"You make it sound sensible."

"That's because it is sensible. Whenever you had sex with a man, you thought about this phantom lover fantasy. Did you have that last night?"

"I don't remember."

"You remember," she said, eyes narrowing. "Did you or didn't you?"

"All right, so I didn't. What does that prove?"

"That you don't need fantasies any more, Ell."

"Then I am a lesbian," Elly Carr said slowly. "That's what you mean, and that's what you've been telling me. And I suppose . . . I guess you're right, aren't you?"

"Yes."

"Then where do we go from here, Maggie?"

Maggie shrugged. "We get dressed," she said. "And we leave this hotel, and take a taxi to Grand Central, and catch the first train to Cheshire Point. You go to your house and I go to my house. And then we wait and see what happens."

"Will we be lovers?"

"I don't know, Ell. We may. You've got to do some thinking, honey. You've got to decide just where you want to wind up. You may hate me."

"I couldn't hate you."

"You might, Ell. You might decide that a lesbian's life is something you couldn't bear to live, that even a secret gay existence is too much for you. And you might repress everything by hating me."

"I wouldn't."

"Maybe not." She shrugged. "It's something you'll work out, Ell. Something you'll resolve on your own."

"So we get dressed now?"

"That's right."

"I see."

Maggie studied the tip of her cigarette. She was doing this stupidly, she thought. She wanted Elly, wanted her desperately, and it would be easier to take advantage of her now, to keep her from sliding back into the heterosexual scheme of things. But she simply wasn't put together that way. Whatever happened, the decision had to be Elly's and it had to be a free one. Otherwise everything would be ruined.

"Mag—"

"What is it, honey?"

"Before we get dressed and go, could we—"

"Could we what?"

"Could we make love?"

"Why . . . oh, God, Ell. Oh, baby!"

"But I don't know what to do," Elly was saying now, the words pouring out in a rush. "I want to. I really want to, but I don't know what to do. Will you help me, Maggie?"

"Oh, God," she breathed. "Yes, Ell. Yes, my baby. Yes, my darling, I'll help you. I'll help you, honey."

CHAPTER 19

All day Tuesday Nan waited for Ted Carr to call.

She didn't know whether to expect the phone or the doorbell to ring. Maybe he would come to her as he had come the day before, ringing her doorbell, telling her to get her clothes off, then making love to her on the living room floor. Maybe he would call instead, to talk to her, to give her instructions on a time and place when and where they could be together. She expected the call rather than his personal appearance, since she couldn't expect him to double back from New York a second day in a row. And she looked forward to the call. She waited to hear his voice, wanted to see what would happen next.

There was one possibility which never occurred to her. She took it for granted that he would contact her, one way or another, and she never conceived of the possibility that he would not call her at all.

He did not call her at all.

She waited until it was quite obvious that he was not calling. She was a few minutes late picking up Skip and Danny at school, and on the way home she barely understood their conversation because she was too busy thinking about Ted. She drove home fast, and while the two of them went downstairs to mesmerize themselves in front of the television set, she sat waiting for the phone to ring.

She almost forgot Ted that night. It was a busy evening; Howard picked up the babysitter at seven, brought the sitter over to help Danny and Skip watch television, and then they went to the inevitable PTA meeting. The meeting was a gigantic bore, complete with a speaker who provided a rather harrowing picture of teenage narcotics addiction. Since Danny and Skip would not be teenagers for awhile, much less narcotics addicts, the speech was not exactly down Nan's alley. Still, it was something to listen to, and while she was at the meeting she hardly thought about Ted Carr at all.

That night she wanted Howard to make love to her. She wanted this very much, but something kept her from putting her desire into words, and Howard did not think of the idea all by himself. He kissed her, and he failed to notice when she pressed up against him a bit more warmly than usual. Then he got into bed and closed his eyes, and before long she heard the rhythmic breathing which told her he was asleep.

But she was not asleep. She stayed awake for hours, thinking about Ted, trying to guess why he hadn't called her. He could have called no matter how busy he was, could at least have said hello to her. Maybe he had just wanted her once. Maybe he was done with her now, and it was time for the boredom to start all over again, and—

She couldn't believe that. She had pleased him—she knew this for a fact—and he would call again, would return soon. And, she decided triumphantly, when he did call she would hang up on him, and when he rang her bell she would shut the door in his face. She could play his game as well as he could. Whether or not she let the affair go on, she was not going to make it easy for him.

She almost believed this.

He didn't call Wednesday, either. She was sure he would call this time, and she put off going shopping in order to be home when he called, but the phone never rang and the doorbell remained silent. Three or four times she walked to the phone, almost ready to dial the number of his New York office, and each time she walked away from the phone, telling herself she was behaving like an idiot and commanding herself to put him out of her mind once and for all.

He called on Thursday.

When the call finally did come, at two-thirty in the afternoon, she had not been expecting it at all. If his aim was to catch her off-base he was succeeding admirably, for she had just about managed to condition herself to the idea that he was never going to contact her again when the phone rang. She picked up the receiver, not even thinking it might be Ted, and his voice said hello to her.

"You didn't call," she said, her resolve to hang up long dissipated. "I was waiting. You didn't call."

"That's right," he said pleasantly. "I didn't."

"I was waiting. But you didn't—"

"You sound like a broken record, Nan-O. I'm at the Star Bright Motel on Route 9. How about getting here as quick as you can?"

"Ted—"

"Unit Six," he went on. "Just come to the door, hurry inside, and pull your panties off. I'm sitting here all ready for you, Nan-O. All ready, kid."

"Ted—"

"Unit Six at the Star Bright Motel. Don't forget."

"Ted, I'm not coming."

A short and sardonic laugh.

"I'm not. I—"

"Of course you are."

"Ted, listen to me. Ted, I'm a wife and a mother—"

More laughter. "You're also a whore and a tramp, Nan-O. I'll be waiting for you."

He hung up on her.

She stood there, her hands knotted into fists, her blood pulsing through her system. I'm not going, she told herself. I'm not going, I don't want to go, I hate the rotten bastard and I'm not going.

She went, of course.

The Star Bright Motel was not a haven for weary travelers. If it had been, the owner might well have starved to death, since his location was hardly ideal in that respect. Travelers heading out of New York would go farther than Westchester before calling it a day, and travelers heading into New York would go all the way in instead of stopping so close to their destination. Still, the Star Bright did a booming business.

In the parlance of the inn-keeper's trade, the Star Bright was a hot-pillow joint. Its occupants were occasionally married, but never to each other. The place was popular for extramarital affairs, equally popular among the younger set that was sufficiently mature to find the back seats of cars uncomfortable.

Otis Wheeler was the owner. Now one would be hard put to

find a more suitable occupation for Otis Wheeler than the one he had. It brought him a good income, and there is certainly nothing wrong with a good income. But there was more to it than that. Otis Wheeler was a voyeur, and there is no place for a voyeur quite so delightful as a hot-pillow joint.

Now it was three on Thursday afternoon, and Otis Wheeler was watching. He was in the little concealed hallway between units five and six, his eyes glued to the piece of one-way glass which was set in the wall of unit six. That had been Otis Wheeler's own special idea. The occupants of the units saw a mirror, while Otis saw them. Why, one couple who had taken a special sort of delight in making love in front of mirrors had justified the expense of installation all by themselves!

But now . . .

The tall man with the sandy hair had been sitting alone, waiting. He sat on a straight-backed chair, which was not unusual. What *was* unusual was the fact that he sat in the chair without any clothes on. He had hung his clothes in the closet.

For awhile Otis thought he was wasting his time watching a lunatic who got his kicks sitting naked in a motel unit. Then the woman came in and Otis knew he was not wasting his time. The woman was blonde, and the woman was pretty, and the woman was stacked like a brick outhouse. Otis liked to watch stacked blondes. He was pleased.

The man sneered, and said something which was probably unpleasant, judging from the expression on his face. The woman cringed. Then, slowly and deliberately, she began to remove her clothes.

Otis watched her. It was not hard to do. The stacked blonde

did a slow strip, and from where he was Otis was able to see everything there was to see. Among other things, he was able to determine that the stacked blonde was genuinely stacked.

The man said something else. The stacked blonde then tried to argue. She opened her mouth and talked back, shaking her blonde head prettily. Whereupon the man seemed to lose his temper.

He appeared to curse. Then he asked something which made the blonde go pale all over. She nodded sadly and sank to her knees. The tall man swung his hand and brought it down hard on her shoulders. It left an ugly red mark.

Otis watched, spellbound, while the tall sandy-haired man spanked the stacked blonde on various interesting portions of her anatomy. Then he said something else and the girl obediently crawled around the floor on all fours, performing various imaginative exercises en route.

She returned, finally, and kneeled before the man—Otis watched. His eyes bugged out. He stared.

CHAPTER 20

When the city-dweller thinks of the country, he thinks of good weather. He imagines summers with a hot sun in a clear sky and a steady breeze blowing, all in contrast to the sooty horror of summer in New York, where the heat is never relieved by breezes and where the tall buildings hold the heat in close and mix it with smoke and sweat. When he thinks of spring in the country he imagines green things coming into bloom, and when he thinks of winter his mind conjures up images of placid unbroken fields of powdery snow. Fall brings images of colored leaves to his mind, and football weather, and brisk air. Winter in New York, on the other hand, means slush; spring means the melting of the slush, and autumn barely exists.

The country-dweller has a somewhat more accurate understanding of these seasonal images of bucolic serenity. He knows that the summer may bring temperatures of 98 in the shade, and that there may well be no shade. He knows that winter can be more than dismal, that snow is wet and cold and needs to be shoveled, that tires skid in it and cars get stuck, and that you can have a coronary shoveling out your driveway. He knows that spring is when the crab grass begins to flourish, and that snow melts in the country in just as revolting a manner as slush melts in city streets, except that it takes longer in the country and that there is more of it.

He knows too that fall, the most nearly acceptable season, can be rainy. He knows that when it rains it pours, and that there are many autumn days in the country that might better be dispensed with.

Friday in Cheshire Point might better have been dispensed with.

The rain had started coming down before dawn would have broken. But dawn didn't really break that day anyway. The sun never really rose; there were too many clouds in the way, all of them black, all of them spilling wetness upon Cheshire Point. There was thunder, and there was lightning, but above all there was rain.

It rained cats and dogs. It rained buckets and barrels and pitchforks. But what it rained most of all was water, and it rained an inordinate quantity of it. It rained and it rained and it rained.

No one really liked the rain. There were a few look-on-the-better-side and every-cold-has-a-cardboard-lining types who told one another that the rain was at least good for the farmers, while the poor farmers sat in their leaky farmhouses and watched their crops get washed out of the ground. Because it was that kind of rain. It was not good for anybody.

The multicolored autumn leaves were picked up and carried along by the rain. They blocked the multicolored autumn sewers, and the rain backed up and filled the multicolored autumn streets of the multicolored autumn towns. Cars plowed through deep water and splashed any poor souls unfortunate and/or stupid enough to be out for a walk.

And it went on raining.

Elly Carr sat by her front window and looked at the rain. There was no poetic ritual of listening to the pitter-patter of tiny raindrops on the window pane. In the first place, the raindrops were not tiny. They were huge, monstrous and montizorous, and there is nothing particularly romantic in a montizorous raindrop. In the second place, montizorous raindrops do not go pitter-patter. They go whoosh, sort of, and they don't fall on a window but lash at it. So Elly Carr sat looking at the rain, and listening to the whoosh of montizorous raindrops against the window pane, and not liking it at all.

She made up a little song and sang it to herself. It went to the tune of "Let's go Barmy, We're in the Army" from the *Three-Penny Opera*. She sang quietly, enjoying herself:

> *Pam's in school and Ted's at work*
> *And here I sit complaining*
> *In front of the window like a jerk*
> *All's dull because it's raining.*

She broke off in the middle of the parody, leaving the window, finding a cigarette and putting a match to it. She smoked silently, trying to get her mind organized. She had not seen Maggie since Tuesday morning, when they had first made love quite magnificently and then had ridden back to the Point on the train. She had talked twice to the redheaded girl on the telephone, but she had not yet been to see her.

The thing was that she had to make a decision, and whichever way she made it, she had a hard life staring her in the face. She was certain now that her lesbianism was a genuine thing, that her only chance for sexual happiness and emotional satisfaction lay in the arms of women, not men. So she was more than willing to continue her homosexual relationship with Maggie Whitcomb.

That was not the problem.

The problem was along those lines of course. The problem lay in the fact that, for the first time, Maggie Whitcomb was wholeheartedly in love. And the type of relationship which Maggie had previously found to be ideal now would not do at all.

"I'm in love with you," Maggie had told her on the phone. "I don't want to share you, Ell. Not with anybody."

That meant no marriage. According to Maggie, she had two choices. They could break up, in which event she would remain with Ted and hide her lesbianism under a nymphomaniacal bushel. Or she could go off with Maggie, divorcing her husband while Maggie divorced Dave, sharing an apartment in Greenwich Village or some similar place, and leading the gay life all the way.

She could not, Maggie had explained, both have and eat her cake. Love would not permit such a relationship. She could be Ted's or Maggie's, but not both.

Which, of course, was a problem.

Because she would have liked to have her cake and eat it as well. She wanted the respectability of marriage to Ted; the idea of leaving mate and child and becoming a sexual pariah did not particularly appeal. But the thought of giving up Maggie and all that Maggie meant was no more appealing. She was caught in a neat little bind, and either way out seemed to be a pitfall, and on top of everything else it was raining.

Hell.

Hell and damnation.

Hell!

"Look at it this way," Maggie had explained, her voice persuasively logical. "We'll be hiding, Ell. Hiding everything, worrying about exposure, playing secret little games. And eventually some prying snooping long-eared nosy son of a bitch will find out, and then we'll be in the worst possible kind of mess. That's no good, Ell."

True enough. That was distinctly no good.

"And we don't have each other, not as well as we should. I don't want to make love to you while I'm looking at my watch. I want you around all the time. I want to go to bed with you at night and wake up with you in the morning. I don't want to share you, not sexually or emotionally. I want you for more than sex, Ell. I'm in love with you."

And, naturally, she was in love with Maggie. She knew how Maggie felt and felt the same way herself. But was she ready to commit herself that completely? Was she ready to toss everything overboard and become a full-time lesbian? Maybe what she was going through was a passing phase, maybe some morning she would open her eyes and discover that lesbianism was less than absurd, that she wanted to sleep with men rather than women.

Maybe—

Hell.

The rain was not letting up. It was getting worse, if that were possible, and Elly thought hysterically that it was going to go on like this for forty days and forty nights. The thing to do, she told herself, was to get busy building an ark. She would make it forty cubits long and thirty cubits deep and twenty cubits wide, and into it she would put two members of each species of every living thing. But she would put in two women of each species. It would be the first lesbian ark in history.

She laughed. Outside the rain kept coming down.

CHAPTER 21

Nan Haskell was taking a bath. There was enough water outside for her to bathe in the yard, but she hadn't gone quite that far yet. Ted was breaking down her reserve, pushing her inhibitions a little further each time, but she had not yet reached the point where she would go out and bathe in the rain.

She rarely took tub baths. She usually preferred showers—they were faster and simpler, and you didn't wind up lolling in a tub of dirty water that way. But this morning she was taking a bath. She was not interested in getting clean, since she had already had her morning shower. She was sitting in a tub of hot water because she ached.

Ached.

Her muscles were sore, and her flesh was sore, and her stomach was weak from throwing up. The little fun-and-games episode at the Star Bright Motel had left her broken and vomiting. It had been one for the books, all things considered.

She never would have believed herself capable of such perverted behavior, never could have imagined herself submitting to such bestiality and, what was more, getting an insane sort of kick out of it. And yet she had submitted, and had gotten those insane kicks, and now her whole body ached.

Ached from the spanking, and from being kicked. And from

throwing up, sick with herself, humiliated and ashamed. She had done things no woman should do, had done them with a man who was evil and twisted and vile. And now she lay in the tub, soaking herself in steaming water, trying to bring herself back to life again.

Maybe she should kill herself.

It was a tempting thought. All you did was take your life and put an end to it, and then all the little worries, along with yourself, simply ceased to be. God, what was the best way to kill yourself? A doctor had assured her once at a party that the simplest and most pleasant suicide method called for a lethal intravenous injection of morphine. This had impressed her at the time, but less than a year later that same doctor had placed the barrel of a shotgun in his mouth, triggered the gun with his toe, and blown his brains all over Westchester County, thus killing himself off in as painful and unappetizing a manner as possible.

> *Razors pain you*
> *Rivers are damp*
> *Acids stain you*
> *And drugs cause cramp.*
> *Guns aren't lawful*
> *Nooses give*
> *Gas smells awful—*
> *You might as well live.*

The poem was one of Dorothy Parker's, and it summed things up precisely enough. She put her head in one hand, thinking now what a cockeyed course events had taken. She'd started out bored, and had entered into an affair with Ted to escape somehow from boredom. And now she was thinking of suicide, which was nothing but the ultimate boredom of death.

It was the town, she thought. Cheshire Point. When all was said and done, the town of Cheshire Point was nothing but a grass-covered tree-shaded trap. You wound up with all the inconveniences of country life and all the pressures of city life, the unpleasantness of either way of life all rolled into one unpalatable pill. You watched your husband go off to the city each morning, and you waited in occupied monotony for him to return, while other women waited in the same manner in all of the other houses in town.

You waited, and you went crazy. You lived in a fundamentally artificial manner, living in the town but not really a part of it, with your social world composed solely of people in your own special niche, other expatriate New Yorkers with the same problems and the same frustrations.

She rubbed her aching shoulders, massaged her sore breasts. Sitting in the tub wasn't really doing a hell of a lot of good, but there didn't seem to be anything else to do. And, if nothing else, the tub was a pleasant place for the analysis of the myriad ills besetting the unidyllic community of Cheshire Point.

But what was she going to do? God, she'd looked for an escape from boredom and had wound up holding a man-eating tiger by the tail. She wasn't bored now, certainly. Monotony would have been a relief.

She had to end the thing with Ted. An illicit love affair would have been bad enough, but, as Ted Carr had told her himself, in this instance love had nothing to do with it. This was sex; worse, it was unnatural, a master-slave relationship that could have hardly been less healthy.

It was making a nervous wreck out of her. The episode at the motel had been pure horror, and if she was any great shakes as a prophet, things could only get progressively worse. Ted would seek to make her more wretched, would strive to find new and improved ways to humiliate and torment her. A bright future, she told herself firmly, it was not.

But then what? Breaking up with Ted would not be easy—he had an emotional hold over her, and she was perceptive enough to realize how strong it was. Still, she could make the break if she put her mind to it. And where would that leave her?

Up the old creek, natch. The boredom would come back, and she'd try to find some other way to escape, and if the other way were not Ted Carr it would probably be no less harmful to her well-being in the long run. Or, if she managed by hook or crook to avoid such a means of escape, she would only succeed in winding up back where she had started, all bottled up in an empty and insufferable world.

Maybe they could move back to New York. They could sell the house, then buy into a decent co-op apartment building on the East Side. That wasn't the worst place in the world to bring up children. There was that one public school, Number Six, which was as good as most private schools. And, if they weren't in that particular district, tuition for the kids at a decent private school would cost less than the taxes they paid on their split-level trap in Westchester. The boys wouldn't have all that fresh air, but Central Park was nearby. And there were more cultural advantages for the kids—museums and lectures and kiddie concerts and special plays.

There were advantages for the children, in a sense. Kids who grew up in Manhattan were sharper than their country cousins, more sophisticated, more keenly polished. They understood more things and tended to develop into more interesting people. Maybe Cheshire Point was a trap for kids, too. Maybe Danny and Skip were being molded into television-watching morons, breathing fresh air but never developing as they might.

Maybe—

Would Howard move back? She realized suddenly that she actually had no idea how he felt about Cheshire Point. And that made her aware of just how little they communicated. He might like the house and he might hate it; she had no way of knowing which was the case, just as he was no doubt unaware of how she felt. They'd grown apart, living in Cheshire Point. In New York they had been very close, but the gracious-living rat-race had separated them, impeding communications and keeping them apart.

Maybe Howard wanted to return to the city himself. Maybe he hated the Point just as she did and would welcome a chance to return to Manhattan. That would solve everything. Oh, there would still be problems—that much was impossible to avoid. But the problems would work themselves out in Manhattan. If you took a pair of people and put them where they really belonged, they had a chance to be happy. If you stuck them in the wrong environment, the chance was smaller.

She got up from the tub, stepped out of it, wrapped herself up in a towel. She massaged her skin with the towel until it glowed, healthy and pink and alive again. She drained the water from the tub, scrubbed the ring away and rinsed the tub out. Then she went to her bedroom and dressed. She got into a simple skirt and sweater and left her feet bare.

She went downstairs, poured a cup of coffee, took it into the living room, sat down with it. She was just beginning to understand exactly how much she loved Howard, how much her husband meant to her. She had pretty much fallen out of love with Howard lately, not because of anything he had done but because they had not been able to sustain in Cheshire Point the sort of relationship they had built up in New York. Love did not grow by itself. It had to be fed and nourished. When you only saw your husband at breakfast and after dinner, when he left the house at dawn and returned at dusk, love was hard to keep going. When you spent your free time partying with people you didn't really like and attending meetings of the Parent-Teacher Association, love could disappear in a sea of trivia and banality.

But the love was real. Howard was her husband and she loved him, loved him more now that a disgusting affair with a disgusting man had showed her just how badly their marital relationship was atrophying.

She wriggled her bare toes, took another sip of hot coffee. New York was a big town; you didn't have to spend time with people whom you didn't happen to like. You could live next door to another couple for twenty years and never say more than hello and nice day to them. You picked your own friends, and you spent your time whatever way you damn pleased, and that was an infinitely saner way of life than exurbia afforded.

She didn't want to kid herself. Manhattan was as much of a rat race as Cheshire Point, perhaps more of one. But it was their kind of rat race, and that made all the difference.

The more she thought about it, the more convinced she became that Howard would go for the idea. He was no happier in the country than she was, and they both belonged back in New York. She would discuss it with him that night; they could do that instead of wasting time at some drunken brawl.

And as far as Ted Carr went, she was not going to waste her time worrying about him. She did not need him any more. He had never been a problem, but was only the symptom of a fundamental ill. When the main problem was solved, Ted would not matter at all.

She walked to the window, looked out. It was still raining.

Roz Barclay went down to the basement to put a load of wash in the washing machine. She put in the recommended low-suds detergent, added bleach, and got things off to a good start. Then she climbed the cellar stairs and found a chair in the living room to sit in.

It was still pouring. There was no justice, she decided. The wonderful thing about being a writer was that you could work at home. You didn't have to rush into the city, and when the weather was rotten you stayed snug as a bug under your own little roof.

So what had happened? Well, it rained. And Linc, who had just finished both *Murder By Moonlight* and a slick story called *One Cup Of Sorrow,* had been stuck with that most miserable day for a run in to New York to deliver both scripts to his agent. It could have been worse, of course. Linc was in considerably higher spirits taking scripts to his agent than cadging advances.

She smiled. The rain was unimportant—Linc wouldn't melt. What was important, and very important, was that he was writing, that the typewriter did what he wanted it to do. She was married, she told herself, to a very special sort of man. He was only half-alive when he was not writing. It was as though that IBM electric in the study were an extension of himself, a natural outgrowth of his hands and arms. Away from it he was not his full self. His moods were intense and unhappy, and he spent his days alternately blaming himself and blaming the world.

But when things went right, then not even rain could spoil the perfection of the day. Then the world was Linc's oyster and she was his pearl, and God was in his heaven and everything was just fine.

So she did not mind the rain.

Linc would be home soon. She checked her watch, counting minutes, waiting for him. He was going to take the rest of the day off—God knew he deserved some time off after the way he'd plowed through the book and the short story. They were going to have dinner out, maybe at The Gables or some similar restaurant, and then they'd come home for a few drinks and a little of the old togetherness routine.

And he was interested in things now. He'd been talking at breakfast about spending the winter in Mexico, insisting that it wouldn't be too much more expensive than staying in the States, that they could combine business with pleasure, taking an apartment in Mexico City or a shack in a small fishing village. Linc would write, as usual, and they would have a ball. Besides, travel was tax deductible for a writer. All he had to do was set a novel in Mexico and they could write off the trip.

That was Linc, she thought. They were broke, advanced to the hilt, and he was planning a trip and justifying it as tax deductible. She wondered whether or not they would go and hoped that they would. Somehow they would get the money, and somehow they would manage to afford it, and it would be nice. Neither of them had ever been to Mexico. It would be a nice change.

She didn't mind the rain at all.

She thought back to the slump now, remembering how bad it had been, remembering things which might better have been forgotten. She pictured herself sitting alone in the bathroom playing auto-erotic games like a sex-crazed teenager, but the image did not cause her to blush or to feel ashamed. She smiled to herself.

Slumps were hard times, hard for her and harder still for Linc. But you had to take the bad with the good, the wheat with the chaff, or something like that. It was like the weather—some days you were going to have rain and you had to accept it. The good times made up for the bad times with plenty of room left over.

Some women, she knew, had it easier. Some men—most men, for that matter—were a good deal easier to live with than Linc was. These were the steady men, the plodding men, the men who made no music and dreamed no dreams. They worked steadily and made love on schedule, and their wives lived an easy life.

That was fine for some women. Roz would have died of boredom.

Because those women did not know what they were missing. They couldn't know the joy that came when your husband cracked through a barrier, when he did something really well and overflowed with satisfaction. They couldn't look back on times like that surprise movie sale, when the two of them danced around like lunatics, staying up all night drinking to Hollywood and money and the times they were going to have together. They couldn't imagine what real happiness was.

She felt sorry for them.

She went to the window. No, she thought, I do not mind the rain. Not at all.

The sunshine makes up for it.

Chapter 22

Elly Carr was the kind of woman who had trouble making decisions. Now she was still at her window, still looking at water and listening to the whoosh of montizorous raindrops against the window, still trying to decide whether to have her cake or eat it, whether to run off with Maggie or stick with Ted.

Alone, she might never have made the decision.

She had help.

She saw the panel truck pull to the curb in front of her house. She tried to read the lettering on its side, but the rain was coming down so thick and so hard that she could not make it out. She saw the man get out of the truck and begin to make the trek through the rain up her driveway to the door. He was halfway to the door before she recognized him. Then her heart skipped a beat.

It was Rudy Gerber.

Rudy Gerber. The brawny and brainless one who delivered for the dry cleaner. But he was not delivering today; his hands were empty. And he was not coming to pick up anything, since this was not the pick-up day.

She shuddered. He was coming to pick up something, all right. He was coming to pick *her* up. And if there was one thing she did not want, it was the physical embrace of Rudy Gerber.

The thought alone made her nauseous.

She wanted to run, to hide. She heard him ring the doorbell and made no move to answer it, hoping against hope that he would go away and leave her alone. But he did not go away and leave her alone. He stayed precisely where he was, on her doorstep, and he went on ringing the damned bell. She thought she was going to go out of her mind.

She thought insanely that she would sit in her chair by the window forever, and that eternity would spin itself out without her answering the door and without his taking a hint and leaving. But finally she stood up on shaky legs and walked to the door. She looked through the little window into his stupid pig eyes. Her hand found the doorknob, turned it, tugged.

The door opened and he came inside.

"I thought I'd give you a break," he said thickly. "Thought I'd take a little time off work to give you a little pleasure. You had me worried when you didn't answer the door."

"Not . . . today," she managed.

He went on as though he hadn't heard her. "Worried," he said. "I thought maybe you was with somebody else. You know, screwing for some other guy."

"I—"

"And then I figured I'd have to sit around and wait for sloppy seconds. You know, take up where the other guy left off. But today's my lucky day, huh? You're all alone. I guess not many guys would've come out in rain like this just for a piece of you. But I'm hungry, Mrs. Carr. I can use a piece of you."

"Get out," she said.

"Huh?"

"I want you to get out."

"I don't getcha . . ."

"That's the whole point," she said levelly. "You don't get me. Not today and not ever. You get the hell out of here and you don't come back. You leave me alone or I call the police."

He scratched his head, genuinely puzzled. Then his pig eyes assumed a crafty expression.

"You wouldn't call no cops," he said. "Not you. I could tell 'em a few things about good old Mrs. Carr that would set 'em on their ears. I could tell the whole town a few things about Mrs. Carr. Nice things. Juicy things. I don't think you'll call no cops."

"Look—"

"And I don't think I'll get outta here just like that," he went on. "You know how that rain's comin' down? You know what it's like out there? I didn't come through that rain for the hell of it. I came because I figured on taking you to bed. And you know something?"

She stared at him.

"I still figure on taking you to bed, Mrs. Carr."

"No—"

He did not take her to bed, if one wishes to be precise. He took her, but on the living room couch rather than on the bed. She did not cooperate. She was raped.

She fought, but a girl her size could hardly expect to put up much of a fight against a man the size of Rudy Gerber. She raked his face with her nails, drawing blood, and she aimed a knee at his groin. But when he drew back a ham-sized fist and struck her savagely in the stomach, the fight went out of her at once. She sagged and fell forward, and he caught her by the shoulders and led her back to the couch.

And raped her.

It took a long time, and it hurt, and it was awful. When it was over she crawled to the upstairs bathroom and showered. Then she threw up a few times and showered again.

Men were rotten.

Men were vile and evil; she did not want them and could not stand them. Men were like Rudy Gerber—they took you whether you wanted to be taken or not, because they were concerned with nothing other than their own self-satisfaction.

Men were no good.

Her decision had not been an easy one to make. Now it had been made for her. Now she knew with certainty that she could not go through life as Ted Carr's wife, that she could not conceivably be married to any man. She was a lesbian, and if that made her abnormal and perverted that was just too damned bad. She knew what she was, and she knew that she could no more go on enduring sex with men that she hated than she could stomach being raped by men like Rudy Gerber.

She went to the phone.

She dialed Maggie's number.

"Throw some clothes in a suitcase," she told Maggie. "In a hurry. I'm going to pack in about five minutes and spend thirty seconds leaving a note for Ted. Then I'm going to hop in the Caddy and come by for you. You'd better be ready."

"That's short notice, Ell."

"That's the way it has to be, Maggie."

"Are you sure you know what you're doing?"

"I'm positive."

A pause.

Then: "I love you, Ell."

"I love you, Maggie."

Nan Haskell fumbled a cigarette loose from her pack and leaned forward to take a light from her husband. She was breathless now: she had been talking, virtually without interruption, for almost half an hour. Now it was Howard's turn to say something.

She waited.

He said: "I think it's a damned fine idea, Nan."

"Do you mean that?"

"I've never meant anything more sincerely. Except when I asked you to marry me. This country life is no good for us, Nan. We're dying out here. We should get back to the city."

"Can we afford it?"

"We'll save money. I've been . . . looking at apartment ads lately. We can buy one hell of a fine co-op for less than half of what we can sell this place for. And the monthly maintenance comes to less than taxes and upkeep on this architectural horror. We'll be way ahead."

"You've been looking at ads?"

He nodded. "I've thought about moving back for weeks now. But I was afraid you liked it here."

"Howie, I hate it!"

"So do I. But I never knew—"

And they started laughing together. They laughed heartily and happily for the first time in far too long. They laughed hysterically, and they held each other close, and they hurried the kids off to bed.

Then they, too, went to bed.

Much later Nan lay awake, ready for sleep but too happy to close her eyes. Everything was going to be all right now, she know. Howard was her husband and she loved him and he loved her. Ted Carr was a horrible mistake who was no longer a part of her life. He had not even left a scar.

Everything was going to be all right now.

The young couple stood at the railway station in Cheshire Point. The man was about twenty-six, with short hair and gray flannel suit. The woman wore a pregnancy outfit, neat maternity clothes which covered a belly due to give forth life in approximately three and one-half months.

They had looked at a house that afternoon. They were city-dwellers and did not own a car, so they were waiting for the train to take them back to New York. The house they had looked over was a swank split-level colonial on a full acre plot of land. They both liked it.

"I think we can afford it," the man was saying. "After all, we'll be paying off the mortgage the same as we're paying rent now. And at the end we'll have something to show for it. It's a beautiful house, isn't it?"

"Lovely. And all that yard for the kids to play in."

"Kids?"

"Well, kid. But kids, eventually. I love it, honey."

The man put an arm around the girl's shoulders. "Just think of it," he said. "Fresh air to breathe. And we'll be able to have a car finally. You know, I miss driving a car. It'll be good to have one again. You can't drive in Manhattan without losing your mind."

"I know."

"I'll like it here."

"It's a long way for you to come for work," the woman said. "Are you sure you won't mind it?"

"I'll enjoy it. Give me a chance to get my brain working in the morning and a chance to unwind at night. I won't walk in grumbling about the hard time they gave me."

"Are you sure you won't mind? I mean, it's an hour or so in the morning and the same thing at night."

"Better than fighting the subway."

"Oh," she said. "I guess you're right. Smell the air, honey! Isn't it divine?"

They sniffed the air together and agreed that it was divine.

"Just one thing," the man said. "You know, you'll be all alone here with not much to do."

"I'll have the baby—"

"Besides that, I mean. What'll you do for friends?"

"I'll have loads of friends," she said. "Women like myself, with husbands who go to New York to work. And they'll be decent, interesting people. Not like that madhouse of a city where you can live next to a person for fifteen years without saying more than hello and goodbye."

"Sure," he agreed. "We'll make real friends here."

"It'll be great."

"Wonderful."

They fell silent, thinking just how wonderful it would be.

"Oh," he said suddenly. "Oh, it's nothing."

"What?"

"Just a thought," he said. "I won't mind it at all."

"Mind what?"

"Well," he said, "it'll probably be pretty . . . quiet here, almost a little dull. I guess not much happens in a little town like Cheshire Point."

"Will you miss the excitement?"

"Not me," he insisted. "How about you?"

She shook her head firmly. "It will be a pleasure," she said. "Just peace and quiet. Because what could ever happen in Cheshire Point?"

My Newsletter: I get out an email newsletter at unpredictable intervals, but rarely more often than every other week. I'll be happy to add you to the distribution list. A blank email to lawbloc@gmail.com with "newsletter" in the subject line will get you on the list, and a click of the "Unsubscribe" link will get you off it, should you ultimately decide you're happier without it.

Lawrence Block has been writing award-winning mystery and suspense fiction for half a century. You can read his thoughts about crime fiction and crime writers in *The Crime of Our Lives*, where this MWA Grand Master tells it straight. His most recent novels are *The Girl With the Deep Blue Eyes*; *The Burglar Who Counted the Spoons*, featuring Bernie Rhodenbarr; *Hit Me*, featuring Keller; and *A Drop of the Hard Stuff*, featuring Matthew Scudder, played by Liam Neeson in the film *A Walk Among the Tombstones*. Several of his other books have been filmed, although not terribly well. He's well known for his books for writers, including the classic *Telling Lies for Fun &f Profit*, and *The Liar's Bible*. In addition to prose works, he has written episodic television (*Tilt!*) and the Wong Kar-wai film, *My Blueberry Nights*. He is a modest and humble fellow, although you would never guess as much from this biographical note.

Email: lawbloc@gmail.com
Twitter: @LawrenceBlock
Facebook: lawrence.block
Website: lawrenceblock.com